Defoe Abbott Marx Hardy Montaigne Machiavelli Chesterton Cooper Emerson Joyce Austen
Melville Hugo Eliot Grimm Molière
Stoker Carroll Christie Haggard Byron Schiller
Wilde Maupassant Engels Smith Kafka
Garnett Einstein Fitzgerald Hawthorne Hall
Goethe Dostoyevsky Willis
Baum Cotton Kipling Doyle
Henry Nietzsche
Leslie Dumas Flaubert Turgenev Balzac Crane
Stockton Vatsyayana Verne Vinci
Curtis Burroughs Gogol Busch
Homer Tocqueville Whitman
Darwin Widger Tolstoy Twain Scott
Potter Freud Thoreau Plato Harte
Kant Zola Lawrence Dickens Hesse
Jowett Stevenson Burton
London Andersen Descartes Cervantes Voltaire
Poe Aristotle Wells Cooke
Hale James Hastings Irving
Bunner Shakespeare Chambers
Richter Dante da Chekhov Benedict Alcott
Doré Swift Shaw Wodehouse Pushkin
Newton

ⓣ tredition®

tredition was established in 2006 by Sandra Latusseck and Soenke Schulz. Based in Hamburg, Germany, tredition offers publishing solutions to authors and publishing houses, combined with world-wide distribution of printed and digital book content. tredition is uniquely positioned to enable authors and publishing houses to create books on their own terms and without conventional manufacturing risks.

For more information please visit: www.tredition.com

TREDITION CLASSICS

This book is part of the TREDITION CLASSICS series. The creators of this series are united by passion for literature and driven by the intention of making all public domain books available in printed format again - worldwide. Most TREDITION CLASSICS titles have been out of print and off the bookstore shelves for decades. At tredition we believe that a great book never goes out of style and that its value is eternal. Several mostly non-profit literature projects provide content to tredition. To support their good work, tredition donates a portion of the proceeds from each sold copy. As a reader of a TREDITION CLASSICS book, you support our mission to save many of the amazing works of world literature from oblivion. See all available books at www.tredition.com.

Project Gutenberg

The content for this book has been graciously provided by Project Gutenberg. Project Gutenberg is a non-profit organization founded by Michael Hart in 1971 at the University of Illinois. The mission of Project Gutenberg is simple: To encourage the creation and distribution of eBooks. Project Gutenberg is the first and largest collection of public domain eBooks.

Old Greek Folk Stories Told Anew

Josephine Preston Peabody

Imprint

This book is part of TREDITION CLASSICS

Author: Josephine Preston Peabody
Cover design: Buchgut, Berlin – Germany

Publisher: tredition GmbH, Hamburg - Germany
ISBN: 978-3-8424-6728-6

www.tredition.com
www.tredition.de

PUBLISHERS' NOTE.

Hawthorne, in his *Wonder-Book* and *Tanglewood Tales*, has told, in a manner familiar to multitudes of American children and to many more who once were children, a dozen of the old Greek folk stories. They have served to render the persons and scenes known as no classical dictionary would make them known. But Hawthorne chose a few out of the many myths which are constantly appealing to the reader not only of ancient but of modern literature. The group contained in the collection which follows will help to fill out the list; it is designed to serve as a complement to the *Wonder-Book* and *Tanglewood Tales*, so that the references to the stories in those collections are brief and allusive only. In order to make the entire series more useful, the index added to this number of the *Riverside Literature Series* is made to include also the stories contained in the other numbers of the series which contain Hawthorne's two books. Thus the index serves as a tolerably full clue to the best-known characters in Greek mythology.

Once upon a time, men made friends with the Earth. They listened to all that woods and waters might say; their eyes were keen to see wonders in silent country places and in the living creatures that had not learned to be afraid. To this wise world outside the people took their joy and sorrow; and because they loved the Earth, she answered them.

It was not strange that Pan himself sometimes brought home a shepherd's stray lamb. It was not strange, if one broke the branches of a tree, that some fair life within wept at the hurt. Even now, the Earth is glad with us in springtime, and we grieve for her when the leaves go. But in the old days there was a closer union, clearer speech between men and all other creatures, Earth and the stars about her.

Out of the life that they lived together, there have come down to us these wonderful tales; and, whether they be told well or ill, they are too good to be forgotten.

CONTENTS

THE WOOD-FOLK

THE JUDGMENT OF MIDAS

PROMETHEUS

THE DELUGE

ORPHEUS AND EURYDICE

ICARUS AND DAEDALUS

PHAETHON

NIOBE

ADMETUS AND THE SHEPHERD

ALCESTIS

APOLLO'S SISTER

I. DIANA AND ACTAEON II. DIANA AND ENDYMION

THE CALYDONIAN HUNT

ATALANTA'S RACE

ARACHNE

PYRAMUS AND THISBE

PYGMALION AND GALATEA

OEDIPUS

CUPID AND PSYCHE

THE TRIAL OF PSYCHE

STORIES OP THE TROJAN WAR

I. THE APPLE OF DISCORD II. THE ROUSING OF THE HEROES III. THE WOODEN HORSE

THE HOUSE OF AGAMEMNON

THE ADVENTURES OF ODYSSEUS

I. THE CURSE OF POLYPHEMUS II. THE WANDERING OF ODYSSEUS III. THE HOME-COMING

THE WOOD-FOLK.

Pan led a merrier life than all the other gods together. He was beloved alike by shepherds and countrymen, and by the fauns and satyrs, birds and beasts, of his own kingdom. The care of flocks and herds was his, and for home he had all the world of woods and waters; he was lord of everything out-of-doors! Yet he felt the burden of it no more than he felt the shadow of a leaf when he danced, but spent the days in laughter and music among his fellows. Like him, the fauns and satyrs had furry, pointed ears, and little horns that sprouted above their brows; in fact, they were all enough like wild creatures to seem no strangers to anything untamed. They slept in the sun, piped in the shade, and lived on wild grapes and the nuts that every squirrel was ready to share with them.

The woods were never lonely. A man might wander away into those solitudes and think himself friendless; but here and there a river knew, and a tree could tell, a story of its own. Beautiful creatures they were, that for one reason or another had left off human shape. Some had been transformed against their will, that they might do no more harm to their fellow-men. Some were changed through the pity of the gods, that they might share the simple life of Pan, mindless of mortal cares, glad in rain and sunshine, and always close to the heart of the Earth.

There was Dryope, for instance, the lotus-tree. Once a careless, happy woman, walking among the trees with her sister Iole and her own baby, she had broken a lotus that held a live nymph hidden, and blood dripped from the wounded plant. Too late, Dryope saw her heedlessness; and there her steps had taken root, and there she had said good-by to her child, and prayed Iole to bring him sometimes to play beneath her shadow. Poor mother-tree! Perhaps she took comfort with the birds and gave a kindly shelter to some nest.

There, too, was Echo, once a wood-nymph who angered the goddess Juno with her waste of words, and was compelled now to wait till others spoke, and then to say nothing but their last word, like any mocking-bird. One day she saw and loved the youth Narcissus, who was searching the woods for his hunting companions. "Come hither!" he called, and Echo cried "Hither!" eager to speak at last. "Here am I,—come!" he repeated, looking about for the voice. "I come," said Echo, and she stood before him. But the youth, angry at such mimicry, only stared at her and hastened away. From that time she faded to a voice, and to this day she lurks hidden and silent till you call.

But Narcissus himself was destined to fall in love with a shadow. For, leaning over the edge of a brook one day, he saw his own beautiful face looking up at him like a water-nymph. He leaned nearer, and the face rose towards him, but when he touched the surface it was gone in a hundred ripples. Day after day he besought the lovely creature to have pity and to speak; but it mocked him with his own tears and smiles, and he forgot all else, until he changed into a flower that leans over to see its image in the pool.

There, too, was the sunflower Clytie, once a maiden who thought nothing so beautiful as the sun-god Phoebus Apollo. All the day long she used to look after him as he journeyed across the heavens in his golden chariot, until she came to be a fair rooted plant that ever turns its head to watch the sun.

Many like were there. Daphne the laurel, Hyacinthus (once a beautiful youth, slain by mischance), who lives and renews his bloom as a flower,—these and a hundred others. The very weeds were friendly....

But there were wise, immortal voices in certain caves and trees. Men called them Oracles; for here the gods spoke in answer to the prayers of folk in sorrow or bewilderment. Sometimes they built a temple around such a befriending voice, and kings would journey far to hear it speak.

As for Pan, only one grief had he, and in the end a glad thing came of it.

One day, when he was loitering in Arcadia, he saw the beautiful wood-nymph Syrinx. She was hastening to join Diana at the chase, and she herself was as swift and lovely as any bright bird that one longs to capture. So Pan thought, and he hurried after to tell her. But Syrinx turned, caught one glimpse of the god's shaggy locks and bright eyes, and the two little horns on his head (he was much like a wild thing, at a look), and she sprang away down the path in terror.

Begging her to listen, Pan followed; and Syrinx, more and more frightened by the patter of his hoofs, never heeded him, but went as fast as light till she came to the brink of the river. Only then she paused, praying her friends, the water-nymphs, for some way of escape. The gentle, bewildered creatures, looking up through the water, could think of but one device.

Just as the god overtook Syrinx and stretched out his arms to her, she vanished like a mist, and he found himself grasping a cluster of tall reeds. Poor Pan!

The breeze that sighed whenever he did—and oftener—shook the reeds and made a sweet little sound,—a sudden music. Pan heard it, half consoled.

"Is it your voice, Syrinx?" he said. "Shall we sing together?"

He bound a number of the reeds side by side; to this day, shepherds know how. He blew across the hollow pipes and they made music!

THE JUDGMENT OF MIDAS

Pan came at length to be such a wonderful piper with his syrinx (for so he named his flute) that he challenged Apollo to make better music if he could. Now the sun-god was also the greatest of divine musicians, and he resolved to punish the vanity of the country-god, and so consented to the test. For judge they chose the mountain Tmolus, since no one is so old and wise as the hills. And, since Tmolus could not leave his home, to him went Pan and Apollo, each with his followers, oreads and dryads, fauns, satyrs, and centaurs.

Among the worshippers of Pan was a certain Midas, who had a strange story. Once a king of great wealth, he had chanced to befriend Dionysus, god of the vine; and when he was asked to choose some good gift in return, he prayed that everything he touched might be turned into gold. Dionysus smiled a little when he heard this foolish prayer, but he granted it. Within two days, King Midas learned the secret of that smile, and begged the god to take away the gift that was a curse. He had touched everything that belonged to him, and little joy did he have of his possessions! His palace was as yellow a home as a dandelion to a bee, but not half so sweet. Row upon row of stiff golden trees stood in his garden; they no longer knew a breeze when they heard it. When he sat down to eat, his feast turned to treasure uneatable. He learned that a king may starve, and he came to see that gold cannot replace the live, warm gifts of the Earth. Kindly Dionysus took back the charm, but from that day King Midas so hated gold that he chose to live far from luxury, among the woods and fields. Even here he was not to go free from misadventure.

Tmolus gave the word, and Pan uprose with his syrinx, and blew upon the reeds a melody so wild and yet so coaxing that the squirrels came, as if at a call, and the birds hopped down in rows. The trees swayed with a longing to dance, and the fauns looked at one another and laughed for joy. To their furry little ears, it was the sweetest music that could be.

But Tmolus bowed before Apollo, and the sun-god rose with his golden lyre in his hands. As he moved, light shook out of his radiant hair as raindrops are showered from the leaves. His trailing robes were purple, like the clouds that temper the glory of a sunset, so that one may look upon it. He touched the strings of his lyre, and all things were silent with joy. He made music, and the woods dreamed. The fauns and satyrs were quite still; and the wild creatures crouched, blinking, under a charm of light that they could not understand. To hear such a music cease was like bidding farewell to father and mother.

With one accord they fell at the feet of Apollo, and Tmolus proclaimed the victory his. Only one voice disputed that award.

Midas refused to acknowledge Apollo lord of music,—perhaps because the looks of the god dazzled his eyes unpleasantly, and put him in mind of his foolish wish years before. For him there was no music in a golden lyre!

But Apollo would not leave such dull ears unpunished. At a word from him they grew long, pointed, furry, and able to turn this way and that (like a poplar leaf),—a plain warning to musicians. Midas had the ears of an ass, for every one to see!

For a long time the poor man hid this oddity with such skill that we might never have heard of it. But one of his servants learned the secret, and suffered so much from keeping it to himself that he had to unburden his mind at last. Out into the meadows he went, hollowed a little place in the turf, whispered the strange news into it quite softly, and heaped the earth over again. Alas! a bed of reeds sprang up there before long, and whispered in turn to the grass-blades. Year after year they grew again, ever gossipping among themselves; and to this day, with every wind that sets them nodding together, they murmur, laughing, *"Midas has the ears of an ass: Oh, hush, hush!"*

PROMETHEUS.

In the early days of the universe, there was a great struggle for empire between Zeus and the Titans. The Titans, giant powers of heaven and earth, were for seizing whatever they wanted, with no more ado than a whirlwind. Prometheus, the wisest of all their race, long tried to persuade them that good counsel would avail more than violence; but they refused to listen. Then, seeing that such rulers would soon turn heaven and earth into chaos again, Prometheus left them to their own devices, and went over to Zeus, whom he aided so well that the Titans were utterly overthrown. Down into Tartarus they went, to live among the hidden fires of the earth; and there they spent a long term of bondage, muttering like storm, and shaking the roots of mountains. One of them was Enceladus, who lay bound under Aetna; and one, Atlas, was made to stand and bear up the weight of the sky on his giant shoulders.

Zeus was left King of gods and men. Like any young ruler, he was eager to work great changes with his new power. Among other plans, he proposed to destroy the race of men then living, and to replace it with some new order of creatures. Prometheus alone heard this scheme with indignation. Not only did he plead for the life of man and save it, but ever after he spent his giant efforts to civilize the race, and to endow it with a wit near to that of gods.

In the Golden Age, men had lived free of care. They took no heed of daily wants, since Zeus gave them all things needful, and the earth brought forth fruitage and harvest without asking the toil of husbandmen. If mortals were light of heart, however, their minds were empty of great enterprise. They did not know how to build or plant or weave; their thoughts never flew far, and they had no wish to cross the sea.

But Prometheus loved earthly folk, and thought that they had been children long enough. He was a mighty workman, with the whole world for a workshop; and little by little he taught men knowledge that is wonderful to know, so that they grew out of their childhood, and began to take thought for themselves. Some people even say that he knew how to make men,—as we make shapes out of clay,—and set their five wits going. However that may be, he was certainly a cunning workman. He taught men first to build huts out of clay, and to thatch roofs with straw. He showed them how to make bricks and hew marble. He taught them numbers and letters, the signs of the seasons, and the coming and going of the stars. He showed them how to use for their healing the simple herbs that once had no care save to grow and be fragrant. He taught them how to till the fields; how to tame the beasts, and set them also to work; how to build ships that ride the water, and to put wings upon them that they may go faster, like birds.

With every new gift, men desired more and more. They set out to see unknown lands, and their ambitions grew with their knowledge. They were like a race of poor gods gifted with dreams of great glory and the power to fashion marvellous things; and, though they had no endless youth to spend, the gods were troubled.

Last of all, Prometheus went up secretly to heaven after the treasure of the immortals. He lighted a reed at the flame of the sun, and brought down the holy fire which is dearest to the gods. For with the aid of fire all things are possible, all arts are perfected.

This was his greatest gift to man, but it was a theft from the immortal gods, and Zeus would endure no more. He could not take back the secret of fire; but he had Prometheus chained to a lofty crag in the Caucasus, where every day a vulture came to prey upon his body, and at night the wound would heal, so that it was ever to suffer again. It was a bitter penalty for so noble-hearted a rebel, and as time went by, and Zeus remembered his bygone services, he would have made peace once more. He only waited till Prometheus should bow his stubborn spirit, but this the son of Titans would not do. Haughty as rock beneath his daily torment, believing that he suffered for the good of mankind, he endured for years.

One secret hardened his spirit. He was sure that the empire of Zeus must fall some day, since he knew of a danger that threatened it. For there was a certain beautiful sea-nymph, Thetis, whom Zeus desired for his wife. (This was before his marriage to Queen Juno.) Prometheus alone knew that Thetis was destined to have a son who should be far greater than his father. If she married some mortal, then, the prophecy was not so wonderful; but if she were to marry the King of gods and men, and her son should be greater than he, there could be no safety for the kingdom. This knowledge Prometheus kept securely hidden; but he ever defied Zeus, and vexed him with dark sayings about a danger that threatened his sovereignty. No torment could wring the secret from him. Year after year, lashed by the storms and scorched by the heat of the sun, he hung in chains and the vulture tore his vitals, while the young Oceanides wept at his feet, and men sorrowed over the doom of their protector.

At last that earlier enmity between the gods and the Titans came to an end. The banished rebels were set free from Tartarus, and they themselves came and besought their brother, Prometheus, to hear the terms of Zeus. For the King of gods and men had promised to pardon his enemy, if he would only reveal this one troublous secret.

In all heaven and earth there was but one thing that marred the new harmony,—this long struggle between Zeus and Prometheus; and the Titan relented. He spoke the prophecy, warned Zeus not to marry Thetis, and the two were reconciled. The hero Heracles (himself an earthly son of Zeus) slew the vulture and set Prometheus free.

But it was still needful that a life should be given to expiate that ancient sin,—the theft of fire. It happened that Chiron, noblest of all the Centaurs (who are half horses and half men), was wandering the world in agony from a wound that he had received by strange mischance. For, at a certain wedding-feast among the Lapithae of Thessaly, one of the turbulent Centaurs had attempted to steal away the bride. A fierce struggle followed, and in the general confusion, Chiron, blameless as he was, had been wounded by a poisoned arrow. Ever tormented with the hurt and never to be healed, the immortal Centaur longed for death, and begged that he might be accepted as an atonement for Prometheus. The gods heard his prayer and took away his pain and his immortality. He died like any wearied man, and Zeus set him as a shining archer among the stars.

So ended a long feud. From the day of Prometheus, men spent their lives in ceaseless enterprise, forced to take heed for food and raiment, since they knew how, and to ply their tasks of art and handicraft, They had taken unresting toil upon them, but they had a wondrous servant at their beck and call, — the bright-eyed fire that is the treasure of the gods.

THE DELUGE.

Even with the gifts of Prometheus, men could not rest content. As years went by, they lost all the innocence of the early world; they grew more and more covetous and evil-hearted. Not satisfied with the fruits of the Earth, or with the fair work of their own hands, they delved in the ground after gold and jewels; and for the sake of treasure nations made war upon each other and hate sprang up in households. Murder and theft broke loose and left nothing sacred.

At last Zeus spoke. Calling the gods together, he said: "Ye see what the Earth has become through the baseness of men. Once they were deserving of our protection; now they even neglect to ask it. I will destroy them with my thunderbolts and make a new race."

But the gods withheld him from this impulse. "For," they said, "let not the Earth, the mother of all, take fire and perish. But seek out some means to destroy mankind and leave her unhurt."

So Zeus unloosed the waters of the world and there was a great flood.

The streams that had been pent in narrow channels, like wild steeds bound to the ploughshare, broke away with exultation; the springs poured down from the mountains, and the air was blind with rain. Valleys and uplands were covered; strange countries were joined in one great sea; and where the highest trees had towered, only a little greenery pricked through the water, as weeds show in a brook.

Men and women perished with the flocks and herds. Wild beasts from the forest floated away on the current with the poor sheep. Birds, left homeless, circled and flew far and near seeking some place of rest, and, finding none, they fell from weariness and died with human folk, that had no wings.

Then for the first time the sea-creatures—nymphs and dolphins— ventured far from their homes, up, up through the swollen waters, among places that they had never seen before,—forests whose like they had not dreamed, towns and deluged farmsteads. They went in and out of drowned palaces, and wondered at the strange ways of men. And in and out the bright fish darted, too, without a fear. Wonderful man was no more. His hearth was empty; and fire, his servant, was dead on earth.

One mountain alone stood high above this ruin. It was Parnassus, sacred to the gods; and here one man and woman had found refuge. Strangely enough, this husband and wife were of the race of the Titans,—Deucalion, a son of Prometheus, and Pyrrha, a child of Epimetheus, his brother; and these alone had lived pure and true of heart.

Warned by Prometheus of the fate in store for the Earth, they had put off from their home in a little boat, and had made the crest of Parnassus their safe harbor.

The gods looked down on these two lonely creatures, and, beholding all their past lives clear and just, suffered them to live on. Zeus bade the rain cease and the floods withdraw.

Once more the rivers sought their wonted channels, and the sea-gods and the nymphs wandered home reluctantly with the sinking seas. The sun came out; and they hastened more eagerly to find cool depths. Little by little the forest trees rose from the shallows as if they were growing anew. At last the surface of the world lay clear to see, but sodden and deserted, the fair fields covered with ooze, the houses rank with moss, the temples cold and lightless.

Deucalion and Pyrrha saw the bright waste of water sink and grow dim and the hills emerge, and the earth show green once more. But even their thankfulness of heart could not make them merry.

"Are we to live on this great earth all alone?" they said. "Ah! if we had but the wisdom and cunning of our fathers, we might make a new race of men to bear us company. But now what remains to us? We have only each other for all our kindred."

"Take heart, dear wife," said Deucalion at length, "and let us pray to the gods in yonder temple."

They went thither hand in hand. It touched their hearts to see the sacred steps soiled with the water-weeds, — the altar without fire; but they entered reverently, and besought the Oracle to help them.

"Go forth," answered the spirit of the place, "with your faces veiled and your robes ungirt; and cast behind you, as ye go, the bones of your mother."

Deucalion and Pyrrha heard with amazement. The strange word was terrible to them.

"We may never dare do this," whispered Pyrrha. "It would be impious to strew our mother's bones along the way."

In sadness and wonder they went out together and took thought, a little comforted by the firmness of the dry earth beneath their feet. Suddenly Deucalion pointed to the ground.

"Behold the Earth, our mother!" said he. "Surely it was this that the Oracle meant. And what should her bones be but the rocks that are a foundation for the clay, and the pebbles that strew the path?"

Uncertain, but with lighter hearts, they veiled their faces, ungirt their garments, and, gathering each an armful of the stones, flung them behind, as the Oracle had bidden.

And, as they walked, every stone that Deucalion flung became a man; and every one that Pyrrha threw sprang up a woman. And the hearts of these two were filled with joy and welcome.

Down from the holy mountain they went, all those new creatures, ready to make them homes and to go about human work. For they were strong to endure, fresh and hardy of spirit, as men and women should be who are true children of our Mother Earth.

ORPHEUS AND EURYDICE.

When gods and shepherds piped and the stars sang, that was the day of musicians! But the triumph of Phoebus Apollo himself was not so wonderful as the triumph of a mortal man who lived on earth, though some say that he came of divine lineage. This was Orpheus, that best of harpers, who went with the Grecian heroes of the great ship Argo in search of the Golden Fleece.

After his return from the quest, he won Eurydice for his wife, and they were as happy as people can be who love each other and every one else. The very wild beasts loved them, and the trees clustered about their home as if they were watered with music. But even the gods themselves were not always free from sorrow, and one day misfortune came upon that harper Orpheus whom all men loved to honor.

Eurydice, his lovely wife, as she was wandering with the nymphs, unwittingly trod upon a serpent in the grass. Surely, if Orpheus had been with her, playing upon his lyre, no creature could have harmed her. But Orpheus came too late. She died of the sting, and was lost to him in the Underworld.

For days he wandered from his home, singing the story of his loss and his despair to the helpless passers-by. His grief moved the very stones in the wilderness, and roused a dumb distress in the hearts of savage beasts. Even the gods on Mount Olympus gave ear, but they held no power over the darkness of Hades.

Wherever Orpheus wandered with his lyre, no one had the will to forbid him entrance; and at length he found unguarded that very cave that leads to the Underworld where Pluto rules the spirits of the dead. He went down without fear. The fire in his living heart found him a way through the gloom of that place. He crossed the Styx, the black river that the gods name as their most sacred oath. Charon, the harsh old ferryman who takes the Shades across, forgot to ask of him the coin that every soul must pay. For Orpheus sang.

There in the Underworld the song of Apollo would not have moved the poor ghosts so much. It would have amazed them, like a star far off that no one understands. But here was a human singer, and he sang of things that grow in every human heart, youth and love and death, the sweetness of the Earth, and the bitterness of losing aught that is dear to us.

Now the dead, when they go to the Underworld, drink of the pool of Lethe; and forgetfulness of all that has passed comes upon them like a sleep, and they lose their longing for the world, they lose their memory of pain, and live content with that cool twilight. But not the pool of Lethe itself could withstand the song of Orpheus; and in the hearts of the Shades all the old dreams awoke wondering. They remembered once more the life of men on Earth, the glory of the sun and moon, the sweetness of new grass, the warmth of their homes, all the old joy and grief that they had known. And they wept.

Even the Furies were moved to pity. Those, too, who were suffering punishment for evil deeds ceased to be tormented for themselves, and grieved only for the innocent Orpheus who had lost Eurydice. Sisyphus, that fraudulent king (who is doomed to roll a monstrous boulder uphill forever), stopped to listen. The daughters of Danaus left off their task of drawing water in a sieve. Tantalus forgot hunger and thirst, though before his eyes hung magical fruits that were wont to vanish out of his grasp, and just beyond reach bubbled the water that was a torment to his ears; he did not hear it while Orpheus sang.

So, among a crowd of eager ghosts, Orpheus came, singing with all his heart, before the king and queen of Hades. And the queen Proserpina wept as she listened and grew homesick, remembering the fields of Enna and the growing of the wheat, and her own beautiful mother, Demeter. Then Pluto gave way.

They called Eurydice and she came, like a young guest unused to the darkness of the Underworld. She was to return with Orpheus, but on one condition. If he turned to look at her once before they reached the upper air, he must lose her again and go back to the world alone.

Rapt with joy, the happy Orpheus hastened on the way, thinking only of Eurydice, who was following him. Past Lethe, across the Styx they went, he and his lovely wife, still silent as a Shade. But the place was full of gloom, the silence weighed upon him, he had not seen her for so long; her footsteps made no sound; and he could hardly believe the miracle, for Pluto seldom relents. When the first gleam of upper daylight broke through the cleft to the dismal world, he forgot all, save that he must know if she still followed. He turned to see her face, and the promise was broken!

She smiled at him forgivingly, but it was too late. He stretched out his arms to take her, but she faded from them, as the bright snow, that none may keep, melts in our very hands. A murmur of farewell came to his ears, — no more. She was gone.

He would have followed, but Charon, now on guard, drove him back. Seven days he lingered there between the worlds of life and death, but after the broken promise, Hades would not listen to his song. Back to the Earth he wandered, though it was sweet to him no longer. He died young, singing to the last, and round about the place where his body rested, nightingales nested in the trees. His lyre was set among the stars; and he himself went down to join Eurydice, unforbidden.

Those two had no need of Lethe, for their life on earth had been wholly fair, and now that they are together they no longer own a sorrow.

ICARUS AND DAEDALUS.

Among all those mortals who grew so wise that they learned the secrets of the gods, none was more cunning than Daedalus.

He once built, for King Minos of Crete, a wonderful Labyrinth of winding ways so cunningly tangled up and twisted around that, once inside, you could never find your way out again without a magic clue. But the king's favor veered with the wind, and one day he had his master architect imprisoned in a tower. Daedalus managed to escape from his cell; but it seemed impossible to leave the island, since every ship that came or went was well guarded by order of the king.

At length, watching the sea-gulls in the air,—the only creatures that were sure of liberty,—he thought of a plan for himself and his young son Icarus, who was captive with him.

Little by little, he gathered a store of feathers great and small. He fastened these together with thread, moulded them in with wax, and so fashioned two great wings like those of a bird. When they were done, Daedalus fitted them to his own shoulders, and after one or two efforts, he found that by waving his arms he could winnow the air and cleave it, as a swimmer does the sea. He held himself aloft, wavered this way and that with the wind, and at last, like a great fledgling, he learned to fly.

Without delay, he fell to work on a pair of wings for the boy Icarus, and taught him carefully how to use them, bidding him beware of rash adventures among the stars. "Remember," said the father, "never to fly very low or very high, for the fogs about the earth would weigh you down, but the blaze of the sun will surely melt your feathers apart if you go too near."

For Icarus, these cautions went in at one ear and out by the other. Who could remember to be careful when he was to fly for the first time? Are birds careful? Not they! And not an idea remained in the boy's head but the one joy of escape.

The day came, and the fair wind that was to set them free. The father bird put on his wings, and, while the light urged them to be gone, he waited to see that all was well with Icarus, for the two could not fly hand in hand. Up they rose, the boy after his father. The hateful ground of Crete sank beneath them; and the country folk, who caught a glimpse of them when they were high above the tree-tops, took it for a vision of the gods,—Apollo, perhaps, with Cupid after him.

At first there was a terror in the joy. The wide vacancy of the air dazed them,—a glance downward made their brains reel. But when a great wind filled their wings, and Icarus felt himself sustained, like a halcyon-bird in the hollow of a wave, like a child uplifted by his mother, he forgot everything in the world but joy. He forgot Crete and the other islands that he had passed over: he saw but vaguely that winged thing in the distance before him that was his father Daedalus. He longed for one draught of flight to quench the thirst of his captivity: he stretched out his arms to the sky and made towards the highest heavens.

Alas for him! Warmer and warmer grew the air. Those arms, that had seemed to uphold him, relaxed. His wings wavered, drooped. He fluttered his young hands vainly,—he was falling,—and in that terror he remembered. The heat of the sun had melted the wax from his wings; the feathers were falling, one by one, like snowflakes; and there was none to help.

He fell like a leaf tossed down the wind, down, down, with one cry that overtook Daedalus far away. When he returned, and sought high and low for the poor boy, he saw nothing but the bird-like feathers afloat on the water, and he knew that Icarus was drowned.

The nearest island he named Icaria, in memory of the child; but he, in heavy grief, went to the temple of Apollo in Sicily, and there hung up his wings as an offering. Never again did he attempt to fly.

PHAETHON.

Once upon a time, the reckless whim of a lad came near to destroying the Earth and robbing the spheres of their wits.

There were two playmates, said to be of heavenly parentage. One was Epaphus, who claimed Zeus as a father; and one was Phaethon, the earthly child of Phoebus Apollo (or Helios, as some name the sun-god). One day they were boasting together, each of his own father, and Epaphus, angry at the other's fine story, dared him to go prove his kinship with the Sun.

Full of rage and humiliation, Phaethon went to his mother, Clymene, where she sat with his young sisters, the Heliades.

"It is true, my child," she said, "I swear it in the light of yonder Sun. If you have any doubt, go to the land whence he rises at morning and ask of him any gift you will; he is your father, and he cannot refuse you."

As soon as might be, Phaethon set out for the country of sunrise. He journeyed by day and by night far into the east, till he came to the palace of the Sun. It towered high as the clouds, glorious with gold and all manner of gems that looked like frozen fire, if that might be. The mighty walls were wrought with images of earth and sea and sky. Vulcan, the smith of the gods, had made them in his workshop (for Mount-Aetna is one of his forges, and he has the central fires of the earth to help him fashion gold and iron, as men do glass). On the doors blazed the twelve signs of the Zodiac, in silver that shone like snow in the sunlight. Phaethon was dazzled with the sight, but when he entered the palace hall he could hardly bear the radiance.

In one glimpse through his half-shut eyes, he beheld a glorious being, none other than Phoebus himself, seated upon a throne. He was clothed in purple raiment, and round his head there shone a blinding light, that enveloped even his courtiers upon the right and upon the left,—the Seasons with their emblems, Day, Month, Year, and the beautiful young Hours in a row. In one glance of those all-seeing eyes, the sun-god knew his child; but in order to try him he asked the boy his errand.

"O my father," stammered Phaethon, "if you are my father indeed," and then he took courage; for the god came down from his throne, put off the glorious halo that hurt mortal eyes, and embraced him tenderly.

"Indeed, thou art my son," said he. "Ask any gift of me and it shall be thine; I call the Styx to witness."

"Ah!" cried Phaethon rapturously. "Let me drive thy chariot for one day!"

For an instant the Sun's looks clouded. "Choose again, my child," said he. "Thou art only a mortal, and this task is mine alone of all the gods. Not Zeus himself dare drive the chariot of the Sun. The way is full of terrors, both for the horses and for all the stars along the roadside, and for the Earth, who has all blessings from me. Listen, and choose again." And therewith he warned Phaethon of all the dangers that beset the way,—the great steep that the steeds must climb, the numbing dizziness of the height, the fierce constellations that breathe out fire, and that descent in the west where the Sun seems to go headlong.

But these counsels only made the reckless boy more eager to win honor of such a high enterprise.

"I will take care; only let me go," he begged.

Now Phoebus' had sworn by the black river Styx, an oath that none of the gods dare break, and he was forced to keep his promise.

Already Aurora, goddess of dawn, had thrown open the gates of the east and the stars were beginning to wane. The Hours came forth to harness the four horses, and Phaethon looked with exultation at the splendid creatures, whose lord he was for a day. Wild, immortal steeds they were, fed with ambrosia, untamed as the winds; their very pet names signified flame, and all that flame can do,—Pyrois, Eoüs, Aethon, Phlegon.

As the lad stood by, watching, Phoebus anointed his face with a philter that should make him strong to endure the terrible heat and light, then set the halo upon his head, with a last word of counsel.

"Follow the road," said he, "and never turn aside. Go not too high or too low, for the sake of heavens and earth; else men and gods will suffer. The Fates alone know whether evil is to come of this. Yet if your heart fails you, as I hope, abide here and I will make the journey, as I am wont to do."

But Phaethon held to his choice and bade his father farewell. He took his place in the chariot, gathered up the reins, and the horses sprang away, eager for the road.

As they went, they bent their splendid necks to see the meaning of the strange hand upon the reins, — the slender weight in the chariot. They turned their wild eyes upon Phaethon, to his secret foreboding, and neighed one to another. This was no master-charioteer, but a mere lad, a feather riding the wind. It was holiday for the horses of the Sun, and away they went.

Grasping the reins that dragged him after, like an enemy, Phaethon looked down from the fearful ascent and saw the Earth far beneath him, dim and fair. He was blind with dizziness and bewilderment. His hold slackened and the horses redoubled their speed, wild with new liberty. They left the old tracks. Before he knew where he was, they had startled the constellations and well-nigh grazed the Serpent, so that it woke from its torpor and hissed.

The steeds took fright. This way and that they went, terrified by the monsters they had never encountered before, shaking out of their silver quiet the cool stars towards the north, then fleeing as far to the south among new wonders. The heavens were full of terror.

Up, far above the clouds, they went, and down again, towards the defenceless Earth, that could not flee from the chariot of the Sun. Great rivers hid themselves in the ground, and mountains were consumed.
Harvests perished like a moth that is singed in a candle-flame.

In vain did Phaethon call to the horses and pull upon the reins. As in a hideous dream, he saw his own Earth, his beautiful home and the home of all men, his kindred, parched by the fires of this mad chariot, and blackening beneath him. The ground cracked open and the sea shrank. Heedless water-nymphs, who had lingered in the shallows, were left gasping like bright fishes. The dryads shrank, and tried to cover themselves from the scorching heat. The poor Earth lifted her withered face in a last prayer to Zeus to save them if he might.

Then Zeus, calling all the gods to witness that there was no other means of safety, hurled his thunderbolt; and Phaethon knew no more.

His body fell through the heavens, aflame like a shooting-star; and the horses of the Sun dashed homeward with the empty chariot.

Poor Clymene grieved sore over the boy's death; but the young Heliades, daughters of the Sun, refused all comfort. Day and night they wept together about their brother's grave by the river, until the gods took pity and changed them all into poplar-trees. And ever after that they wept sweet tears of amber, clear as sunlight.

NIOBE.

There are so many tales of the vanity of kings and queens that the half of them cannot be told.

There was Cassiopaeia, queen of Aethiopia, who boasted that her beauty outshone the beauty of all the sea-nymphs, so that in anger they sent a horrible sea-serpent to ravage the coast. The king prayed of an Oracle to know how the monster might be appeased, and learned that he must offer up his own daughter, Andromeda. The maiden was therefore chained to a rock by the sea-side, and left to her fate. But who should come to rescue her but a certain young hero, Perseus, who was hastening homeward after a perilous adventure with the snaky-haired Gorgons. Filled with pity at the story of Andromeda, he waited for the dragon, met and slew him, and set the maiden free. As for the boastful queen, the gods forgave her, and at her death she was set among the stars. That story ended well.

But there was once a queen of Thebes, Niobe, fortunate above all women, and yet arrogant in the face of the gods. Very beautiful she was, and nobly born, but above all things she boasted of her children, for she had seven sons and seven daughters.

Now there came the day when the people were wont to celebrate the feast of Latona, mother of Apollo and Diana; and Niobe, as she stood looking upon the worshippers on their way to the temple, was filled with overweening pride.

"Why do you worship Latona before me?" she cried out. "What does she possess that I have not in greater abundance? She has but two children, while I have seven sons and as many daughters. Nay, if she robbed me out of envy, I should still be rich. Go back to your houses; you have not eyes to know the rightful goddess."

Such impiety was enough to frighten any one, and her subjects returned to their daily work, awestruck and silent.

But Apollo and Diana were filled with wrath at this insult to their divine mother. Not only was she a great goddess and a power in the heavens, but during her life on earth she had suffered many hardships for their sake. The serpent Python had been sent to torment her; and, driven from land to land, under an evil spell, beset with dangers, she had found no resting-place but the island of Delos, held sacred ever after to her and her children. Once she had even been refused water by some churlish peasants, who could not believe in a goddess if she appeared in humble guise and travel-worn. But these men were all changed into frogs.

It needed no word from Latona herself to rouse her children to vengeance. Swift as a thought, the two immortal archers, brother and sister, stood in Thebes, upon the towers of the citadel. Near by, the youth were pursuing their sports, while the feast of Latona went neglected. The sons of Queen Niobe were there, and against them Apollo bent his golden bow. An arrow crossed the air like a sunbeam, and without a word the eldest prince fell from his horse. One by one his brothers died by the same hand, so swiftly that they knew not what had befallen them, till all the sons of the royal house lay slain. Only the people of Thebes, stricken with terror, bore the news to Queen Niobe, where she sat with her seven daughters. She would not believe in such a sorrow.

"Savage Latona," she cried, lifting her arms against the heavens, "never think that you have conquered. I am still the greater."

At that moment one of her daughters sank beside her. Diana had sped an arrow from her bow that is like the crescent moon. Without a cry, nay, even as they murmured words of comfort, the sisters died, one by one. It was all as swift and soundless as snowfall.

Only the guilty mother was left, transfixed with grief. Tears flowed from her eyes, but she spoke not a word, her heart never softened; and at last she turned to stone, and the tears flowed down her cold face forever.

ADMETUS AND THE SHEPHERD.

Apollo did not live always free of care, though he was the most glorious of the gods. One day, in anger with the Cyclopes who work at the forges of Vulcan, he sent his arrows after them, to the wrath of all the gods, but especially of Zeus. (For the Cyclopes always make his thunderbolts, and make them well.) Even the divine arch-er could not go unpunished, and as a penalty he was sent to serve some mortal for a year. Some say one year and some say nine, but in those days time passed quickly; and as for the gods, they took no heed of it.

Now there was a certain king in Thessaly, Admetus by name, and there came to him one day a stranger, who asked leave to serve about the palace. None knew his name, but he was very comely, and moreover, when they questioned him he said that he had come from a position of high trust. So without further delay they made him chief shepherd of the royal flocks.

Every day thereafter, he drove his sheep to the banks of the river Amphrysus, and there he sat to watch them browse. The country-folk that passed drew near to wonder at him, without daring to ask questions. He seemed to have a knowledge of leech-craft, and knew how to cure the ills of any wayfarer with any weed that grew near by; and he would pipe for hours in the sun. A simple-spoken man he was, yet he seemed to know much more than he would say, and he smiled with a kindly mirth when the people wished him sunny weather.

Indeed, as days went by, it seemed as if summer had come to stay, and, like the shepherd, found the place friendly. Nowhere else were the flocks so white and fair to see, like clouds loitering along a bright sky; and sometimes, when he chose, their keeper sang to them. Then the grasshoppers drew near and the swans sailed close to the river banks, and the country-men gathered about to hear wonderful tales of the slaying of the monster Python, and of a king with ass's ears, and of a lovely maiden, Daphne, who grew into a laurel-tree. In time the rumor of these things drew the king himself to listen; and Admetus, who had been to see the world in the ship Argo, knew at once that this was no earthly shepherd, but a god. From that day, like a true king, he treated his guest with reverence and friendliness, asking no questions; and the god was well pleased.

Now it came to pass that Admetus fell in love with a beautiful maiden, Alcestis, and, because of the strange condition that her father Pelias had laid upon all suitors, he was heavy-hearted. Only that man who should come to woo her in a chariot drawn by a wild boar and a lion might ever marry Alcestis; and this task was enough to puzzle even a king.

As for the shepherd, when he heard of it he rose, one fine morning, and left the sheep and went his way, — no one knew whither. If the sun had gone out, the people could not have been more dismayed. The king himself went, late in the day, to walk by the river Amphrysus, and wonder if his gracious keeper of the flocks had deserted him in a time of need. But at that very moment, whom should he see returning from the woods but the shepherd, glorious as sunset, and leading side by side a lion and a boar, as gentle as two sheep! The very next morning, with joy and gratitude, Admetus set out in his chariot for the kingdom of Pelias, and there he wooed and won Alcestis, the most loving wife that was ever heard of.

It was well for Admetus that he came home with such a comrade, for the year was at an end, and he was to lose his shepherd. The strange man came to take leave of the king and queen whom he had befriended.

"Blessed be your flocks, Admetus," he said, smiling. "They shall prosper even though I leave them. And, because you can discern the gods that come to you in the guise of wayfarers, happiness shall never go far from your home, but ever return to be your guest. No man may live on earth forever, but this one gift have I obtained for you. When your last hour draws near, if any one shall be willing to meet it in your stead, he shall die, and you shall live on, more than the mortal length of days. Such kings deserve long life."

So ended the happy year when Apollo tended sheep.

ALCESTIS.

For many years the remembrance of Apollo's service kept Thessaly full of sunlight. Where a god could work, the people took heart to work also. Flocks and herds throve, travellers were befriended, and men were happy under the rule of a happy king and queen.

But one day Admetus fell ill, and he grew weaker and weaker until he lay at death's door. Then, when no remedy was found to help him and the hope of the people was failing, they remembered the promise of the Fates to spare the king if some one else would die in his stead. This seemed a simple matter for one whose wishes are law, and whose life is needed by all his fellow-men. But, strange to say, the substitute did not come forward at once.

Among the king's most faithful friends, many were afraid to die. Men said that they would gladly give their lives in battle, but that they could not die in bed at home like helpless old women. The wealthy had too much to live for; and the poor, who possessed nothing but life, could not bear to give up that. Even the aged parents of Admetus shrunk from the thought of losing the few years that remained to them, and thought it impious that any one should name such a sacrifice.

All this time, the three Fates were waiting to cut the thread of life, and they could not wait longer.

Then, seeing that even the old and wretched clung to their gift of life, who should offer herself but the young and lovely queen, Alcestis? Sorrowful but resolute, she determined to be the victim, and made ready to die for the sake of her husband.

She took leave of her children and commended them to the care of Admetus. All his pleading could not change the decree of the Fates. Alcestis prepared for death as for some consecration. She bathed and anointed her body, and, as a mortal illness seized her, she lay down to die, robed in fair raiment, and bade her kindred farewell. The household was filled with mourning, but it was too late. She waned before the eyes of the king, like daylight that must be gone.

At this grievous moment Heracles, mightiest of all men, who was journeying on his way to new adventures, begged admittance to the palace, and inquired the cause of such grief in that hospitable place. He was told of the misfortune that had befallen Admetus, and, struck with pity, he resolved to try what his strength might do for this man who had been a friend of gods.

Already Death had come out of Hades for Alcestis, and as Heracles stood at the door of her chamber he saw that awful form leading away the lovely spirit of the queen, for the breath had just departed from her body. Then the might that he had from his divine father Zeus stood by the hero. He seized Death in his giant arms and wrestled for victory.

Now Death is a visitor that comes and goes. He may not tarry in the upper world; its air is not for him; and at length, feeling his power give way, he loosed his grasp of the queen, and, weak with the struggle, made escape to his native darkness of Hades.

In the chamber where the royal kindred were weeping, the body of Alcestis lay, fair to see, and once more the breath stirred in her heart, like a waking bird. Back to its home came her lovely spirit, and for long years after she lived happily with her husband, King Admetus.

APOLLO'S SISTER.

I. DIANA AND ACTAEON.

Like the Sun-god, whom men dreaded as the divine archer and loved as the divine singer, Diana, his sister, had two natures, as different as day from night.

On earth she delighted in the wild life of the chase, keeping holiday among the dryads, and hunting with all those nymphs that loved the boyish pastime. She and her maidens shunned the fellowship of men and would not hear of marriage, for they disdained all household arts; and there are countless tales of their cruelty to suitors.

Syrinx and Atalanta were of their company, and Arethusa, who was changed into a fountain and ever pursued by Alpheus the river-god, till at last the two were united. There was Daphne, too, who disdained the love of Apollo himself, and would never listen to a word of his suit, but fled like Syrinx, and prayed like Syrinx for escape; but Daphne was changed into a fair laurel-tree, held sacred by Apollo forever after.

All these maidens were as untamed and free of heart as the wild creatures they loved to hunt, and whoever molested them did so at his peril. None dared trespass in the home of Diana and her nymphs, not even the riotous fauns and satyrs who were heedless enough to go a-swimming in the river Styx, if they had cared to venture near such a dismal place. But the maiden goddess laid a spell upon their unruly wits, even as the moon controls the tides of the sea. Her precincts were holy. There was one man, however, whose ill-timed curiosity brought heavy punishment upon him. This was Actaeon, a grandson of the great king Cadmus.

Wearied with hunting, one noon, he left his comrades and idled through the forest, perhaps to spy upon those woodland deities of whom he had heard. Chance brought him to the very grove where Diana and her nymphs were wont to bathe. He followed the bright thread of the brook, never turning aside, though mortal reverence should have warned him that the place was for gods. The air was wondrous clear and sweet; a throng of fair trees drooped their branches in the way, and from a sheltered grotto beyond fell a mingled sound of laughter and running waters. But Actaeon would not turn back. Roughly pushing aside the laurel branches that hid the entrance of the cave, he looked in, startling Diana and her maidens. In an instant a splash of water shut his eyes, and the goddess, reading his churlish thought, said: "Go now, if thou wilt, and boast of this intrusion."

He turned to go, but a stupid bewilderment had fallen upon him. He looked back to speak, and could not. He put his hand to his head, and felt antlers branching above his forehead. Down he fell on hands and feet; these likewise changed. The poor offender! Crouching by the brook that he had followed, he looked in, and saw nothing but the image of a stag, bending to drink, as only that morning he had seen the creature they had come out to kill. With an impulse of terror he fled away, faster than he had ever run before, crashing through bush and bracken, the noise of his own flight ever after him like an enemy.

Suddenly he heard the blast of a horn close by, then the baying of hounds. His comrades, who had rested and were ready for the chase, made after him. This time he was their prey. He tried to call and could not. His antlers caught in the branches, his breath came with pain, and the dogs were upon him,—his own dogs!

With all the eagerness that he had often praised in them, they fell upon him, knowing not their own master. And so he perished, hunter and hunted.

Only the goddess of the chase could have devised so terrible a revenge.

II. DIANA AND ENDYMION.

But with the daylight, all of Diana's joy in the wild life of the woods seemed to fade. By night, as goddess of the moon, she watched over the sleep of the earth,—measured the tides of the ocean, and went across the wide path of heaven, slow and fair to see. And although she bore her emblem of the bow, like a silver crescent, she was never terrible, but beneficent and lovely.

Indeed, there was once a young shepherd, Endymion, who used to lead his flocks high up the slopes of Mount Latmos to the purer air; and there, while the sheep browsed, he spent his days and nights dreaming on the solitary uplands. He was a beautiful youth and very lonely. Looking down one night from the heavens near by and as lonely as he, Diana saw him, and her heart was moved to tenderness for his weariness and solitude. She cast a spell of sleep upon him, with eternal youth, white and untroubled as moonlight. And there, night after night, she watched his sheep for him, like any peasant maid who wanders slowly through the pastures after the flocks, spinning white flax from her distaff as she goes, alone and quite content.

Endymion dreamed such beautiful dreams as come only to happy poets. Even when he woke, life held no care for him, but he seemed to walk in a light that was for him alone. And all this time, just as the Sun-god watched over the sheep of King Admetus, Diana kept the flocks of Endymion, but it was for love's sake.

THE CALYDONIAN HUNT.

In that day of the chase, there was one enterprise renowned above all others, — the great hunt of Calydon. Thither, in search of high adventure, went all the heroes of Greece, just as they joined the quest of the Golden Fleece, and, in a later day, went to the rescue of Fair Helen in the Trojan War.

For Oeneus, king of Calydon, had neglected the temples of Diana, and she had sent a monstrous boar to lay waste all the fields and farms in the country. The people had never seen so terrible a beast, and they soon wished that they had never offended the goddess who keeps the woods clear of such monsters. No mortal device availed against it, and, after a hundred disasters, Prince Meleager, the son of Oeneus, summoned the heroes to join him in this perilous hunt.

The prince had a strange story. Soon after his birth, Althea, the queen, had seen in a vision the three Fates spinning the thread of life and crooning over their work. For Clotho spins the thread, Lachesis draws it out, and Atropos waits to cut it off with her glittering shears. So the queen beheld them, and heard them foretell that her baby should live no longer than a brand that was then burning on the hearth. Horror inspired the mother. Quick as a thought she seized the brand, put out the flame, and laid it by in some safe and secret place where no harm could touch it. So the child gathered strength and grew up to manhood.

He was a mighty hunter, and the other heroes came gladly to bear him company. Many of the Argonauts were there, — Jason, Theseus, Nestor, even Atalanta, that valorous maiden who had joined the rowers of the Argo, a beloved charge of Diana. Boyish in her boldness for wild sports, she was fleet of foot and very lovely to behold, altogether a bride for a princely hunter. So Meleager thought, the moment that he saw her face.

Together they all set out for the lair of the boar, the heroes and the men of Calydon,—Meleager and his two uncles. Phlexippus and Toxeus, brothers of Queen Althea.

All was ready. Nets were stretched from tree to tree, and the dogs were let loose. The heroes lay in wait. Suddenly the monster, startled by the shouts of the company, rose hideous and unwieldy from his hiding-place and rushed upon them. What were hounds to such as he, or nets spread for a snare? Jason's spear missed and fell. Nestor only saved his life by climbing the nearest tree. Several of the heroes were gored by the tusks of the boar before they could make their escape. In the midst of this horrible tumult, Atalanta sped an arrow at the creature and wounded him. Meleager saw it with joy, and called upon the others to follow. One by one they tried without success, but he, after one false thrust, drove his spear into the side of the monster and laid him dead.

The heroes crowded to do him honor, but he turned to Atalanta, who had first wounded the boar, and awarded her the shaggy hide that was her fair-won trophy. This was too much for the warriors, who had been outdone by a girl. Phlexippus and Toxeus were so enraged that they snatched the prize from the maiden, churlishly, and denied her victory. Maddened at this, Meleager forgot everything but the insult offered to Atalanta, and he fell upon the two men and stabbed them. Only when they lay dead before him did he remember that they were his own kinsmen.

In the mean time news had flown to the city that the pest was slain, and Queen Althea was on her way to the temple to give thanks for their deliverance. At the very gates she came upon a multitude of men surrounding a litter, and drawing near she saw the bodies of her two brothers. Swift upon this horror came a greater shock,—the name of the murderer, her own son Meleager. All pity left the mother's heart when she heard it; she thought only of revenge. In a lightning-flash she remembered that brand which she had plucked from the fire when her son was but a new-born babe,— the brand that was to last with his life.

She ordered a pyre to be built and lighted, and straightway she went to that hiding-place where she had kept the precious thing all these, years, and brought it back and stood before the flames. At the last moment her soul was torn between love for her son and grief for her murdered brothers. She stretched forth the brand, and plucked it again from the tongues of fire. She cried out in despair that the honor of her house should require such an expiation. But, covering her eyes, she flung the brand into the flames.

At the same time, far away with his companions, and unwitting of these things, Meleager was struck through with a sudden pang. Wondering and helpless, the heroes gathered about, to behold him dying of some unknown agony, while he strove to conquer his pain. Even as the brand burned in the fire before the wretched queen, Meleager was consumed by a mysterious death, blessing with his last breath friends and kindred, his dear Atalanta, and the mother who had brought him to this doom, though he knew it not. At last the brand fell into ashes, and in the forest the hero lay dead.

The king and queen fell into such grief when all was known, that Diana took pity upon them and changed them into birds.

ATALANTA'S RACE.

Even if Prince Meleager had lived, it is doubtful if he could ever have won Atalanta to be his wife. The maiden was resolved to live unwed, and at last she devised a plan to be rid of all her suitors. She was known far and wide as the swiftest runner of her time; and so she said that she would only marry that man who could outstrip her in the race, but that all who dared to try and failed must be put to death.

This threat did not dishearten all of the suitors, however, and to her grief, for she was not cruel, they held her to her promise. On a certain day the few bold men who were to try their fortune made ready, and chose young Hippomenes as judge. He sat watching them before the word was given, and sadly wondered that any brave man should risk his life merely to win a bride. But when Atalanta stood ready for the contest, he was amazed by her beauty. She looked like Hebe, goddess of young health, who is a glad serving-maiden to the gods when they sit at feast.

The signal was given, and, as she and the suitors darted away, flight made her more enchanting than ever. Just as a wind brings sparkles to the water and laughter to the trees, haste fanned her loveliness to a glow.

Alas for the suitors! She ran as if Hermes had lent her his winged sandals. The young men, skilled as they were, grew heavy with weariness and despair. For all their efforts, they seemed to lag like ships in a calm, while Atalanta flew before them in some favoring breeze—and reached the goal!

To the sorrow of all on-lookers, the suitors were led away; but the judge himself, Hippomenes, rose and begged leave to try his fortune. As Atalanta listened, and looked at him, her heart was filled with pity, and she would willingly have let him win the race to save him from defeat and death; for he was comely and younger than the others. But her friends urged her to rest and make ready, and she consented, with an unwilling heart.

Meanwhile Hippomenes prayed within himself to Venus: "Goddess of Love, give ear, and send me good speed. Let me be swift to win as I have been swift to love her."

Now Venus, who was not far off,—for she had already moved the heart of Hippomenes to love,—came to his side invisibly, slipped into his hand three wondrous golden apples, and whispered a word of counsel in his ear.

The signal was given; youth and maiden started over the course. They went so like the wind that they left not a footprint. The people cheered on Hippomenes, eager that such valor should win. But the course was long, and soon fatigue seemed to clutch at his throat, the light shook before his eyes, and, even as he pressed on, the maiden passed him by.

At that instant Hippomenes tossed ahead one of the golden apples. The rolling bright thing caught Atalanta's eye, and full of wonder she stooped to pick it up. Hippomenes ran on. As he heard the flutter of her tunic close behind him, he flung aside another golden apple, and another moment was lost to the girl. Who could pass by such a marvel? The goal was near and Hippomenes was ahead, but once again Atalanta caught up with him, and they sped side by side like two dragon-flies. For an instant his heart failed him; then, with a last prayer to Venus, he flung down the last apple. The maiden glanced at it, wavered, and would have left it where it had fallen, had not Venus turned her head for a second and given her a sudden wish to possess it. Against her will she turned to pick up the golden apple, and Hippomenes touched the goal.

So he won that perilous maiden; and as for Atalanta, she was glad to marry such a valorous man. By this time she understood so well what it was like to be pursued, that she had lost a little of her pleasure in hunting.

ARACHNE.

Not among mortals alone were there contests of skill, nor yet among the gods, like Pan and Apollo. Many sorrows befell men because they grew arrogant in their own devices and coveted divine honors. There was once a great hunter, Orion, who outvied the gods themselves, till they took him away from his hunting-grounds and set him in the heavens, with his sword and belt, and his hound at his heels. But at length jealousy invaded even the peaceful arts, and disaster came of spinning!

There was a certain maiden of Lydia, Arachne by name, renowned throughout the country for her skill as a weaver. She was as nimble with her fingers as Calypso, that nymph who kept Odysseus for seven years in her enchanted island. She was as untiring as Penelope, the hero's wife, who wove day after day while she watched for his return. Day in and day out, Arachne wove too. The very nymphs would gather about her loom, naiads from the water and dryads from the trees.

"Maiden," they would say, shaking the leaves or the foam from their hair, in wonder, "Pallas Athena must have taught you!"

But this did not please Arachne. She would not acknowledge herself a debtor, even to that goddess who protected all household arts, and by whose grace alone one had any skill in them.

"I learned not of Athena," said she, "If she can weave better, let her come and try."

The nymphs shivered at this, and an aged woman, who was looking on, turned to Arachne.

"Be more heedful of your words, my daughter," said she. "The goddess may pardon you if you ask forgiveness, but do not strive for honors with the immortals."

Arachne broke her thread, and the shuttle stopped humming.

"Keep your counsel," she said. "I fear not Athena; no, nor any one else."

As she frowned at the old woman, she was amazed to see her change suddenly into one tall, majestic, beautiful,—a maiden of gray eyes and golden hair, crowned with a golden helmet. It was Athena herself.

The bystanders shrank in fear and reverence; only Arachne was unawed and held to her foolish boast.

In silence the two began to weave, and the nymphs stole nearer, coaxed by the sound of the shuttles, that seemed to be humming with delight over the two webs,—back and forth like bees.

They gazed upon the loom where the goddess stood plying her task, and they saw shapes and images come to bloom out of the wondrous colors, as sunset clouds grow to be living creatures when we watch them. And they saw that the goddess, still merciful, was spinning, as a warning for Arachne, the pictures of her own triumph over reckless gods and mortals.

In one corner of the web she made a story of her conquest over the sea-god Poseidon. For the first king of Athens had promised to dedicate the city to that god who should bestow upon it the most useful gift. Poseidon gave the horse. But Athena gave the olive,—means of livelihood,—symbol of peace and prosperity, and the city was called after her name. Again she pictured a vain woman of Troy, who had been turned into a crane for disputing the palm of beauty with a goddess. Other corners of the web held similar images, and the whole shone like a rainbow.

Meanwhile Arachne, whose head was quite turned with vanity, embroidered her web with stories against the gods, making light of Zeus himself and of Apollo, and portraying them as birds and beasts. But she wove with marvellous skill; the creatures seemed to breathe and speak, yet it was all as fine as the gossamer that you find on the grass before rain.

Athena herself was amazed. Not even her wrath at the girl's insolence could wholly overcome her wonder. For an instant she stood entranced; then she tore the web across, and three times she touched Arachne's forehead with her spindle.

"Live on, Arachne," she said. "And since it is your glory to weave, you and yours must weave forever." So saying, she sprinkled upon the maiden a certain magical potion.

Away went Arachne's beauty; then her very human form shrank to that of a spider, and so remained. As a spider she spent all her days weaving and weaving; and you may see something like her handiwork any day among the rafters.

PYRAMUS AND THISBE.

Venus did not always befriend true lovers, as she had befriended Hippomenes, with her three golden apples. Sometimes, in the enchanted island of Cyprus, she forgot her worshippers far away, and they called on her in vain.

So it was in the sad story of Hero and Leander, who lived on opposite borders of the Hellespont. Hero dwelt at Sestos, where she served as a priestess, in the very temple of Venus; and Leander's home was in Abydos, a town on the opposite shore. But every night this lover would swim across the water to see Hero, guided by the light which she was wont to set in her tower. Even such loyalty could not conquer fate. There came a great storm, one night, that put out the beacon, and washed Leander's body up with the waves to Hero, and she sprang into the water to rejoin him, and so perished.

Not wholly unlike this was the fate of Halcyone, a queen of Thessaly, who dreamed that her husband Ceyx had been drowned, and on waking hastened to the shore to look for him. There she saw her dream come true,—his lifeless body floating towards her on the tide; and as she flung herself after him, mad with grief, the air upheld her and she seemed to fly. Husband and wife were changed into birds; and there on the very water, at certain seasons, they build a nest that floats unhurt,—a portent of calm for many days and safe voyage for the ships. So it is that seamen love these birds and look for halcyon weather.

But there once lived in Babylonia two lovers named Pyramus and Thisbe, who were parted by a strange mischance. For they lived in adjoining houses; and although their parents had forbidden them to marry, these two had found a means of talking together through a crevice in the wall.

Here, again and again, Pyramus on his side of the wall and Thisbe on hers, they would meet to tell each other all that had happened

during the day, and to complain of their cruel parents. At length
they decided that they would endure it no longer, but that they
would leave their homes and be married, come what might. They
planned to meet, on a certain evening, by a mulberry-tree near the
tomb of King Ninus, outside the city gates. Once safely met, they
were resolved to brave fortune together.

So far all went well. At the appointed time, Thisbe, heavily veiled,
managed to escape from home unnoticed, and after a stealthy journey through the streets of Babylon, she came to the grove of mul-
berries near the tomb of Ninus. The place was deserted, and once
there she put off the veil from her face to see if Pyramus waited
anywhere among the shadows. She heard the sound of a footfall
and turned to behold—not Pyramus, but a creature unwelcome to
any tryst—none other than a lioness crouching to drink from the
pool hard by.

Without a cry, Thisbe fled, dropping her veil as she ran. She
found a hiding-place among the rocks at some distance, and there
she waited, not knowing what else to do.

The lioness, having quenched her thirst (after some ferocious
meal), turned from the spring and, coming upon the veil, sniffed at
it curiously, tore and tossed it with her reddened jaws,—as she
would have done with Thisbe herself,—then dropped the plaything
and crept away to the forest once more.

It was but a little after this that Pyramus came hurrying to the
meeting-place, breathless with eagerness to find Thisbe and tell her
what had delayed him. He found no Thisbe there. For a moment he
was confounded. Then he looked about for some sign of her, some
footprint by the pool. There was the trail of a wild beast in the grass,
and near by a woman's veil, torn and stained with blood; he caught
it up and knew it for Thisbe's.

So she had come at the appointed hour, true to her word; she had
waited there for him alone and defenceless, and she had fallen a
prey to some beast from the jungle! As these thoughts rushed upon
the young man's mind, he could endure no more.

"Was it to meet me, Thisbe, that you came to such a death!" cried he. "And I followed all too late. But I will atone. Even now I come lagging, but by no will of mine!"

So saying, the poor youth drew his sword and fell upon it, there at the foot of that mulberry-tree which he had named as the trysting-place, and his life-blood ran about the roots.

During these very moments, Thisbe, hearing no sound and a little reassured, had stolen from her hiding-place and was come to the edge of the grove. She saw that the lioness had left the spring, and, eager to show her lover that she had dared all things to keep faith, she came slowly, little by little, back to the mulberry-tree.

She found Pyramus there, according to his promise. His own sword was in his heart, the empty scabbard by his side, and in his hand he held her veil still clasped. Thisbe saw these things as in a dream, and suddenly the truth awoke her. She saw the piteous mischance of all; and when the dying Pyramus opened his eyes and fixed them upon her, her heart broke. With the same sword she stabbed herself, and the lovers died together.

There the parents found them, after a weary search, and they were buried together in the same tomb. But the berries of the mulberry-tree turned red that day, and red they have remained ever since.

PYGMALION AND GALATEA.

The island of Cyprus was dear to the heart of Venus. There her temples were kept with honor, and there, some say, she watched with the Loves and Graces over the long enchanted sleep of Adonis. This youth, a hunter whom she had dearly loved, had died of a wound from the tusk of a wild boar; but the bitter grief of Venus had won over even the powers of Hades. For six months of every year, Adonis had to live as a Shade in the world of the dead; but for the rest of time he was free to breathe the upper air. Here in Cyprus the people came to worship him as a god, for the sake of Venus who loved him; and here, if any called upon her, she was like to listen.

Now there once lived in Cyprus a young sculptor, Pygmalion by name, who thought nothing on earth so beautiful as the white marble folk that live without faults and never grow old. Indeed, he said that he would never marry a mortal woman, and people began to think that his daily life among marble creatures was hardening his heart altogether.

But it chanced that Pygmalion fell to work upon an ivory statue of a maiden, so lovely that it must have moved to envy every breathing creature that came to look upon it. With a happy heart the sculptor wrought day by day, giving it all the beauty of his dreams, until, when the work was completed, he felt powerless to leave it. He was bound to it by the tie of his highest aspiration, his most perfect ideal, his most patient work.

Day after day the ivory maiden looked down at him silently, and he looked back at her until he felt that he loved her more than anything else in the world. He thought of her no longer as a statue, but as the dear companion of his life; and the whim grew upon him like an enchantment. He named her Galatea, and arrayed her like a princess; he hung jewels about her neck, and made all his home beautiful and fit for such a presence.

Now the festival of Venus was at hand, and Pygmalion, like all who loved Beauty, joined the worshippers. In the temple victims were offered, solemn rites were held, and votaries from many lands came to pray the favor of the goddess. At length Pygmalion himself approached the altar and made his prayer.

"Goddess," he said, "who hast vouchsafed to me this gift of beauty, give me a perfect love, likewise, and let me have for bride, one like my ivory maiden." And Venus heard.

Home to his house of dreams went the sculptor, loath to be parted for a day from his statue, Galatea. There she stood, looking down upon him silently, and he looked back at her. Surely the sunset had shed a flush of life upon her whiteness.

He drew near in wonder and delight, and felt, instead of the chill air that was wont to wake him out of his spell, a gentle warmth around her, like the breath of a plant. He touched her hand, and it yielded like the hand of one living! Doubting his senses, yet fearing to reassure himself, Pygmalion kissed the statue.

In an instant the maiden's face bloomed like a waking rose, her hair shone golden as returning sunlight; she lifted her ivory eyelids and smiled at him. The statue herself had awakened, and she stepped down from the pedestal, into the arms of her creator, alive!

There was a dream that came true.

OEDIPUS.

Behind the power of the gods and beyond all the efforts of men, the three Fates sat at their spinning.

No one could tell whence these sisters were, but by some strange necessity they spun the web of human life and made destinies without knowing why. It was not for Clotho to decree whether the thread of a life should be stout or fragile, nor for Lachesis to choose the fashion of the web; and Atropos herself must sometimes have wept to cut a life short with her shears, and let it fall unfinished. But they were like spinners for some Power that said of life, as of a garment, *Thus it must be*. That Power neither gods nor men could withstand.

There was once a king named Laius (a grandson of Cadmus himself), who ruled over Thebes, with Jocasta his wife. To them an Oracle had foretold that if a son of theirs lived to grow up, he would one day kill his father and marry his own mother. The king and queen resolved to escape such a doom, even at terrible cost. Accordingly Laius gave his son, who was only a baby, to a certain herdsman, with instructions to put him to death.

This was not to be. The herdsman carried the child to a lonely mountain-side, but once there, his heart failed him. Hardly daring to disobey the king's command, yet shrinking from murder, he hung the little creature by his feet to the branches of a tree, and left him there to die.

But there chanced to come that way with his flocks, a man who served King Polybus of Corinth. He found the baby perishing in the tree, and, touched with pity, took him home to his master. The king and queen of Corinth were childless, and some power moved them to take this mysterious child as a gift. They called him Oedipus (Swollen-Foot) because of the wounds they had found upon him, and, knowing naught of his parentage, they reared him as their own son. So the years went by.

Now, when Oedipus had come to manhood, he went to consult the Oracle at Delphi, as all great people were wont, to learn what fortune had in store for him. But for him the Oracle had only a sentence of doom. According to the Fates, he would live to kill his own father and wed his mother.

Filled with dismay, and resolved in his turn to conquer fate, Oedipus fled from Corinth; for he had never dreamed that his parents were other than Polybus and Merope the queen. Thinking to escape crime, he took the road towards Thebes, so hastening into the very arms of his evil destiny.

It happened that King Laius, with one attendant, was on his way to Delphi from the city Thebes. In a narrow road he met this strange young man, also driving in a chariot, and ordered him to quit the way. Oedipus, who had been reared to princely honors, refused to obey; and the king's charioteer, in great anger, killed one of the young man's horses. At this insult Oedipus fell upon master and servant; mad with rage, he slew them both, and went on his way, not knowing the half of what he had done. The first saying of the Oracle was fulfilled.

But the prince was to have his day of triumph before the doom. There was a certain wonderful creature called the Sphinx, which had been a terror to Thebes for many days. In form half woman and half lion, she crouched always by a precipice near the highway, and put the same mysterious question to every passer-by. None had ever been able to answer, and none had ever lived to warn men of the riddle; for the Sphinx fell upon every one as he failed, and hurled him down the abyss, to be dashed in pieces.

This way came Oedipus towards the city Thebes, and the Sphinx crouched, face to face with him, and spoke the riddle that none had been able to guess.

"What animal is that which in the morning goes on four feet, at noon on two, and in the evening upon three?"

Oedipus, hiding his dread of the terrible creature, took thought, and answered "Man. In childhood he creeps on hands and knees, in manhood he walks erect, but in old age he has need of a staff."

At this reply the Sphinx uttered a cry, sprang headlong from the rock into the valley below, and perished. Oedipus had guessed the answer. When he came to the city and told the Thebans that their torment was gone, they hailed him as a deliverer. Not long after, they married him with great honor to their widowed queen, Jocasta, his own mother. The destiny was fulfilled.

For years Oedipus lived in peace, unwitting; but at length upon that unhappy city there fell a great pestilence and famine. In his distress the king sent to the Oracle at Delphi, to know what he or the Thebans had done, that they should be so sorely punished. Then for the third time the Oracle spoke his own fateful sentence; and he learned all.

Jocasta died, and Oedipus took the doom upon himself, and left Thebes. Blinded by his own hand, he wandered away into the wilderness. Never again did he rule over men; and he had one only comrade, his faithful daughter Antigone. She was the truest happiness in his life of sorrow, and she never left him till he died.

CUPID AND PSYCHE.

Once upon a time, through that Destiny that overrules the gods, Love himself gave up his immortal heart to a mortal maiden. And thus it came to pass.

There was a certain king who had three beautiful daughters. The two elder married princes of great renown; but Psyche, the youngest, was so radiantly fair that no suitor seemed worthy of her. People thronged to see her pass through the city, and sang hymns in her praise, while strangers took her for the very goddess of beauty herself.

This angered Venus, and she resolved to cast down her earthly rival. One day, therefore, she called hither her son Love (Cupid, some name him), and bade him sharpen his weapons. He is an archer more to be dreaded than Apollo, for Apollo's arrows take life, but Love's bring joy or sorrow for a whole life long.

"Come, Love," said Venus. "There is a mortal maid who robs me of my honors in yonder city. Avenge your mother. Wound this precious Psyche, and let her fall in love with some churlish creature mean in the eyes of all men."

Cupid made ready his weapons, and flew down to earth invisibly. At that moment Psyche was asleep in her chamber; but he touched her heart with his golden arrow of love, and she opened her eyes so suddenly that he started (forgetting that he was invisible), and wounded himself with his own shaft.

Heedless of the hurt, moved only by the loveliness of the maiden, he hastened to pour over her locks the healing joy that he ever kept by him, undoing all his work. Back to her dream the princess went, unshadowed by any thought of love. But Cupid, not so light of heart, returned to the heavens, saying not a word of what had passed.

Venus waited long; then, seeing that Psyche's heart had somehow escaped love, she sent a spell upon the maiden. From that time, lovely as she was, not a suitor came to woo; and her parents, who desired to see her a queen at least, made a journey to the Oracle, and asked counsel.

Said the voice: "The princess Psyche shall never wed a mortal. She shall be given to one who waits for her on yonder mountain; he overcomes gods and men."

At this terrible sentence the poor parents were half distraught, and the people gave themselves up to grief at the fate in store for their beloved princess. Psyche alone bowed to her destiny. "We have angered Venus unwittingly," she said, "and all for sake of me, heedless maiden that I am! Give me up, therefore, dear father and mother. If I atone, it may be that the city will prosper once more."

So she besought them, until, after many unavailing denials, the parents consented; and with a great company of people they led Psyche up the mountain, — as an offering to the monster of whom the Oracle had spoken, — and left her there alone.

Full of courage, yet in a secret agony of grief, she watched her kindred and her people wind down the mountain-path, too sad to look back, until they were lost to sight. Then, indeed, she wept, but a sudden breeze drew near, dried her tears, and caressed her hair, seeming to murmur comfort. In truth, it was Zephyr, the kindly West Wind, come to befriend her; and as she took heart, feeling some benignant presence, he lifted her in his arms, and carried her on wings as even as a sea-gull's, over the crest of the fateful mountain and into a valley below. There he left her, resting on a bank of hospitable grass, and there the princess fell asleep.

When she awoke, it was near sunset. She looked about her for some sign of the monster's approach; she wondered, then, if her grievous trial had been but a dream. Near by she saw a sheltering forest, whose young trees seemed to beckon as one maid beckons to another; and eager for the protection of the dryads, she went thither.

The call of running waters drew her farther and farther, till she came out upon an open place, where there was a wide pool. A fountain fluttered gladly in the midst of it, and beyond there stretched a white palace wonderful to see. Coaxed by the bright promise of the place, she drew near, and, seeing no one, entered softly. It was all kinglier than her father's home, and as she stood in wonder and awe, soft airs stirred about her. Little by little the silence grew murmurous like the woods, and one voice, sweeter than the rest, took words. "All that you see is yours, gentle high princess," it said. "Fear nothing; only command us, for we are here to serve you."

Full of amazement and delight, Psyche followed the voice from hall to hall, and through the lordly rooms, beautiful with everything that could delight a young princess. No pleasant thing was lacking. There was even a pool, brightly tiled and fed with running waters, where she bathed her weary limbs; and after she had put on the new and beautiful raiment that lay ready for her, she sat down to break her fast, waited upon and sung to by the unseen spirits.

Surely he whom the Oracle had called her husband was no monster, but some beneficent power, invisible like all the rest. When daylight waned he came, and his voice, the beautiful voice of a god, inspired her to trust her strange destiny and to look and long for his return. Often she begged him to stay with her through the day, that she might see his face; but this he would not grant.

"Never doubt me, dearest Psyche," said he. "Perhaps you would fear if you saw me, and love is all I ask. There is a necessity that keeps me hidden now. Only believe."

So for many days Psyche was content; but when she grew used to happiness, she thought once more of her parents mourning her as lost, and of her sisters who shared the lot of mortals while she lived as a goddess. One night she told her husband of these regrets, and begged that her sisters at least might come to see her. He sighed, but did not refuse.

"Zephyr shall bring them hither," said he. And on the following morning, swift as a bird, the West Wind came over the crest of the high mountain and down into the enchanted valley, bearing her two sisters.

They greeted Psyche with joy and amazement, hardly knowing how they had come hither. But when this fairest of the sisters led them through her palace and showed them all the treasures that were hers, envy grew in their hearts and choked their old love. Even while they sat at feast with her, they grew more and more bitter; and hoping to find some little flaw in her good fortune, they asked a thousand questions.

"Where is your husband?" said they. "And why is he not here with you?"

"Ah," stammered Psyche. "All the day long—he is gone, hunting upon the mountains."

"But what does he look like?" they asked; and Psyche could find no answer.

When they learned that she had never seen him, they laughed her faith to scorn.

"Poor Psyche," they said. "You are walking in a dream. Wake, before it is too late. Have you forgotten what the Oracle decreed,—that you were destined for a dreadful creature, the fear of gods and men? And are you deceived by this show of kindliness? We have come to warn you. The people told us, as we came over the mountain, that your husband is a dragon, who feeds you well for the present, that he may feast the better, some day soon. What is it that you trust? Good words! But only take a dagger some night, and when the monster is asleep go, light a lamp, and look at him. You can put him to death easily, and all his riches will be yours—and ours."

Psyche heard this wicked plan with horror. Nevertheless, after her sisters were gone, she brooded over what they had said, not seeing their evil intent; and she came to find some wisdom in their words. Little by little, suspicion ate, like a moth, into her lovely mind; and at nightfall, in shame and fear, she hid a lamp and a dagger in her chamber. Towards midnight, when her husband was fast asleep, up she rose, hardly daring to breathe; and coming softly to his side, she uncovered the lamp to see some horror.

But there the youngest of the gods lay sleeping,—most beautiful, most irresistible of all immortals. His hair shone golden as the sun, his face was radiant as dear Springtime, and from his shoulders sprang two rainbow wings.

Poor Psyche was overcome with self-reproach. As she leaned towards him, filled with worship, her trembling hands held the lamp ill, and some burning oil fell upon Love's shoulder and awakened him.

He opened his eyes, to see at once his bride and the dark suspicion in her heart.

"O doubting Psyche!" he exclaimed with sudden grief, — and then he flew away, out of the window.

Wild with sorrow, Psyche tried to follow, but she fell to the ground instead. When she recovered her senses, she stared about her. She was alone, and the place was beautiful no longer. Garden and palace had vanished with Love.

THE TRIAL OF PSYCHE.

Over mountains and valleys Psyche journeyed alone until she came to the city where her two envious sisters lived with the princes whom they had married. She stayed with them only long enough to tell the story of her unbelief and its penalty. Then she set out again to search for Love.

As she wandered one day, travel-worn but not hopeless, she saw a lofty palace on a hill near by, and she turned her steps thither. The place seemed deserted. Within the hall she saw no human being,— only heaps of grain, loose ears of corn half torn from the husk, wheat and barley, alike scattered in confusion on the floor. Without delay, she set to work binding the sheaves together and gathering the scattered ears of corn in seemly wise, as a princess would wish to see them. While she was in the midst of her task, a voice startled her, and she looked up to behold Demeter herself, the goddess of the harvest, smiling upon her with good will.

"Dear Psyche," said Demeter, "you are worthy of happiness, and you may find it yet. But since you have displeased Venus, go to her and ask her favor. Perhaps your patience will win her pardon."

These motherly words gave Psyche heart, and she reverently took leave of the goddess and set out for the temple of Venus. Most humbly she offered up her prayer, but Venus could not look at her earthly beauty without anger.

"Vain girl," said she, "perhaps you have come to make amends for the wound you dealt your husband; you shall do so. Such clever people can always find work!"

Then she led Psyche into a great chamber heaped high with mingled grain, beans, and lintels (the food of her doves), and bade her separate them all and have them ready in seemly fashion by night. Heracles would have been helpless before such a vexatious task; and poor Psyche, left alone in this desert of grain, had not courage to begin. But even as she sat there, a moving thread of black crawled across the floor from a crevice in the wall; and bending nearer, she saw that a great army of ants in columns had come to her aid. The zealous little creatures worked in swarms, with such industry over the work they like best, that, when Venus came at night, she found the task completed.

"Deceitful girl," she cried, shaking the roses out of her hair with impatience, "this is my son's work, not yours. But he will soon forget you. Eat this black bread if you are hungry, and refresh your dull mind with sleep. To-morrow you will need more wit."

Psyche wondered what new misfortune could be in store for her. But when morning came, Venus led her to the brink of a river, and, pointing to the wood across the water, said, "Go now to yonder grove where the sheep with the golden fleece are wont to browse. Bring me a golden lock from every one of them, or you must go your ways and never come back again."

This seemed not difficult, and Psyche obediently bade the goddess farewell, and stepped into the water, ready to wade across. But as Venus disappeared, the reeds sang louder and the nymphs of the river, looking up sweetly, blew bubbles to the surface and murmured: "Nay, nay, have a care, Psyche. This flock has not the gentle ways of sheep. While the sun burns aloft, they are themselves as fierce as flame; but when the shadows are long, they go to rest and sleep, under the trees; and you may cross the river without fear and pick the golden fleece off the briers in the pasture."

Thanking the water-creatures, Psyche sat down to rest near them, and when the time came, she crossed in safety and followed their counsel. By twilight she returned to Venus with her arms full of shining fleece.

"No mortal wit did this," said Venus angrily. "But if you care to prove your readiness, go now, with this little box, down to Proserpina and ask her to enclose in it some of her beauty, for I have grown pale in caring for my wounded son."

It needed not the last taunt to sadden Psyche. She knew that it was not for mortals to go into Hades and return alive; and feeling that Love had forsaken her, she was minded to accept her doom as soon as might be.

But even as she hastened towards the descent, another friendly voice detained her. "Stay, Psyche, I know your grief. Only give ear and you shall learn a safe way through all these trials." And the voice went on to tell her how one might avoid all the dangers of Hades and come out unscathed. (But such a secret could not pass from mouth to mouth, with the rest of the story.)

"And be sure," added the voice, "when Proserpina has returned the box, not to open it, however much you may long to do so."

Psyche gave heed, and by this device, whatever it was, she found her way into Hades safely, and made her errand known to Proserpina, and was soon in the upper world again, wearied but hopeful.

"Surely Love has not forgotten me," she said. "But humbled as I am and worn with toil, how shall I ever please him? Venus can never need all the beauty in this casket; and since I use it for Love's sake, it must be right to take some." So saying, she opened the box, heedless as Pandora! The spells and potions of Hades are not for mortal maids, and no sooner had she inhaled the strange aroma than she fell down like one dead, quite overcome.

But it happened that Love himself was recovered from his wound, and he had secretly fled from his chamber to seek out and rescue Psyche. He found her lying by the wayside; he gathered into the casket what remained of the philter, and awoke his beloved.

"Take comfort," he said, smiling. "Return to our mother and do her bidding till I come again."

Away he flew; and while Psyche went cheerily homeward, he hastened up to Olympus, where all the gods sat feasting, and begged them to intercede for him with his angry mother.

They heard his story and their hearts were touched. Zeus himself coaxed Venus with kind words till at last she relented, and remembered that anger hurt her beauty, and smiled once more. All the younger gods were for welcoming Psyche at once, and Hermes was sent to bring her hither. The maiden came, a shy newcomer among those bright creatures. She took the cup that Hebe held out to her, drank the divine ambrosia, and became immortal.

Light came to her face like moonrise, two radiant wings sprang from her shoulders; and even as a butterfly bursts from its dull cocoon, so the human Psyche blossomed into immortality.

Love took her by the hand, and they were never parted any more.

STORIES OF THE TROJAN WAR.

I. THE APPLE OF DISCORD.

There was once a war so great that the sound of it has come ringing down the centuries from singer to singer, and will never die.

The rivalries of men and gods brought about many calamities, but none so heavy as this; and it would never have come to pass, they say, if it had not been for jealousy among the immortals,—all because of a golden apple! But Destiny has nurtured ominous plants from little seeds; and this is how one evil grew great enough to overshadow heaven and earth.

The sea-nymph Thetis (whom Zeus himself had once desired for his wife) was given in marriage to a mortal, Peleus, and there was a great wedding-feast in heaven. Thither all the immortals were bidden, save one, Eris, the goddess of Discord, ever an unwelcome guest. But she came unbidden. While the wedding-guests sat at feast, she broke in upon their mirth, flung among them a golden apple, and departed with looks that boded ill. Some one picked up the strange missile and read its inscription: *For the Fairest*; and at once discussion arose among the goddesses. They were all eager to claim the prize, but only three persisted.

Venus, the very goddess of beauty, said that it was hers by right; but Juno could not endure to own herself less fair than another, and even Athena coveted the palm of beauty as well as of wisdom, and would not give it up! Discord had indeed come to the wedding-feast. Not one of the gods dared to decide so dangerous a question,—not Zeus himself, —and the three rivals were forced to choose a judge among mortals.

Now there lived on Mount Ida, near the city of Troy, a certain young shepherd by the name of Paris. He was as comely as Ganymede himself,—that Trojan youth whom Zeus, in the shape of an eagle, seized and bore away to Olympus, to be a cup-bearer to the gods. Paris, too, was a Trojan of royal birth, but like Oedipus he had been left on the mountain in his infancy, because the Oracle had foretold that he would be the death of his kindred and the ruin of his country. Destiny saved and nurtured him to fulfil that prophecy. He grew up as a shepherd and tended his flocks on the mountain, but his beauty held the favor of all the wood-folk there and won the heart of the nymph Oenone.

To him, at last, the three goddesses entrusted the judgment and the golden apple. Juno first stood before him in all her glory as Queen of gods and men, and attended by her favorite peacocks as gorgeous to see as royal fan-bearers.

"Use but the judgment of a prince, Paris," she said, "and I will give thee wealth and kingly power."

Such majesty and such promises would have moved the heart of any man; but the eager Paris had at least to hear the claims of the other rivals. Athena rose before him, a vision welcome as daylight, with her sea-gray eyes and golden hair beneath a golden helmet.

"Be wise in honoring me, Paris," she said, "and I will give thee wisdom that shall last forever, great glory among men, and renown in war."

Last of all, Venus shone upon him, beautiful as none can ever hope to be. If she had come, unnamed, as any country maid, her loveliness would have dazzled him like sea-foam in the sun; but she was girt with her magical Cestus, a spell of beauty that no one can resist.

Without a bribe she might have conquered, and she smiled upon his dumb amazement, saying, "Paris, thou shalt yet have for wife the fairest woman in the world."

At these words, the happy shepherd fell on his knees and offered her the golden apple. He took no heed of the slighted goddesses, who vanished in a cloud that boded storm.

From that hour he sought only the counsel of Venus, and only cared to find the highway to his new fortunes. From her he learned that he was the son of King Priam of Troy, and with her assistance he deserted the nymph Oenone, whom he had married, and went in search of his royal kindred.

For it chanced at that time that Priam proclaimed a contest of strength between his sons and certain other princes, and promised as prize the most splendid bull that could be found among the herds of Mount Ida. Thither came the herdsmen to choose, and when they led away the pride of Paris's heart, he followed to Troy, thinking that he would try his fortune and perhaps win back his own.

The games took place before Priam and Hecuba and all their children, including those noble princes Hector and Helenus, and the young Cassandra, their sister. This poor maiden had a sad story, in spite of her royalty; for, because she had once disdained Apollo, she was fated to foresee all things, and ever to have her prophecies disbelieved. On this fateful day, she alone was oppressed with strange forebodings.

But if he who was to be the ruin of his country had returned, he had come victoriously. Paris won the contest. At the very moment of his honor, poor Cassandra saw him with her prophetic eyes; and seeing as well all the guilt and misery that he was to bring upon them, she broke into bitter lamentations, and would have warned her kindred against the evil to come. But the Trojans gave little heed; they were wont to look upon her visions as spells of madness. Paris had come back to them a glorious youth and a victor; and when he made known the secret of his birth, they cast the words of the Oracle to the winds, and received the shepherd as a long-lost prince.

Thus far all went happily. But Venus, whose promise had not yet been fulfilled, bade Paris procure a ship and go in search of his destined bride. The prince said nothing of this quest, but urged his kindred to let him go; and giving out a rumor that he was to find his father's lost sister Hesione, he set sail for Greece, and finally landed at Sparta.

There he was kindly received by Menelaus, the king, and his wife,
Fair
Helen.

This queen had been reared as the daughter of Tyndarus and Queen Leda, but some say that she was the child of an enchanted swan, and there was indeed a strange spell about her. All the greatest heroes of Greece had wooed her before she left her father's palace to be the wife of King Menelaus; and Tyndarus, fearing for her peace, had bound her many suitors by an oath. According to this pledge, they were to respect her choice, and to go to the aid of her husband if ever she should be stolen away from him. For in all Greece there was nothing so beautiful as the beauty of Helen. She was the fairest woman in the world.

Now thus did Venus fulfil her promise and the shepherd win his reward with dishonor. Paris dwelt at the court of Menelaus for a long time, treated with a royal courtesy which he ill repaid. For at length while the king was absent on a journey to Crete, his guest won the heart of Fair Helen, and persuaded her to forsake her husband and sail away to Troy.

King Menelaus returned to find the nest empty of the swan. Paris and the fairest woman in the world were well across the sea.

II. THE ROUSING OF THE HEROES.

When this treachery came to light, all Greece took fire with indignation. The heroes remembered their pledge, and wrath came upon them at the wrong done to Menelaus. But they were less angered with Fair Helen than with Paris, for they felt assured that the queen had been lured from her country and out of her own senses by some spell of enchantment. So they took counsel how they might bring back Fair Helen to her home and husband.

Years had come and gone since that wedding-feast when Eris had flung the apple of discord, like a firebrand, among the guests. But the spark of dissension that had smouldered so long burst into flame now, and, fanned by the enmities of men and the rivalries of the gods, it seemed like to fire heaven and earth.

A few of the heroes answered the call to arms unwillingly. Time had reconciled them to the loss of Fair Helen, and they were loath to leave home and happiness for war, even in her cause.

One of these was Odysseus, king of Ithaca, who had married Penelope, and was quite content with his kingdom and his little son

Telemachus. Indeed, he was so unwilling to leave them that he feigned madness in order to escape service, appeared to forget his own kindred, and went ploughing the seashore and sowing salt in the furrows. But a messenger, Palamedes, who came with the summons to war, suspected that this sudden madness might be a stratagem, for the king was far famed as a man of many devices. He therefore stood by, one day (while Odysseus, pretending to take no heed of him, went ploughing the sand), and he laid the baby Telemachus directly in the way of the ploughshare. For once the wise man's craft deserted him. Odysseus turned the plough sharply, caught up the little prince, and there his fatherly wits were manifest! After this he could no longer play madman. He had to take leave of his beloved wife Penelope and set out to join the heroes, little dreaming that he was not to return for twenty years. Once embarked, however, he set himself to work in the common cause of the heroes, and was soon as ingenious as Palamedes in rousing laggard warriors.

There remained one who was destined to be the greatest warrior of all. This was Achilles, the son of Thetis,—foretold in the day of Prometheus as a man who should far outstrip his own father in glory and greatness. Years had passed since the marriage of Thetis to King Peleus, and their son Achilles was now grown to manhood, a wonder of strength indeed, and, moreover, invulnerable. For his mother, forewarned of his death in the Trojan War, had dipped him in the sacred river Styx when he was a baby, so that he could take no hurt from any weapon. From head to foot she had plunged him in, only forgetting the little heel that she held him by, and this alone could be wounded by any chance. But even with such precautions Thetis was not content. Fearful at the rumors of war to be, she had her son brought up, in woman's dress, among the daughters of King Lycomedes of Scyros, that he might escape the notice of men and cheat his destiny.

To this very palace, however, came Odysseus in the guise of a merchant, and he spread his wares before the royal household,— jewels and ivory, fine fabrics, and curiously wrought weapons. The king's daughters chose girdles and veils and such things as women delight in; but Achilles, heedless of the like, sought out the weapons, and handled them with such manly pleasure that his nature stood revealed. So he, too, yielded to his destiny and set out to join the heroes.

Everywhere men were banded together, building the ships and gathering supplies. The allied forces of Greece (the Achaeans, as they called themselves) chose Agamemnon for their commander-in-chief. He was a mighty man, king of Mycenae and Argos, and the brother of the wronged Menelaus. Second to Achilles in strength was the giant Ajax; after him Diomedes, then wise Odysseus, and Nestor, held in great reverence because of his experienced age and fame. These were the chief heroes. After two years of busy preparation, they reached the port of Aulis, whence they were to sail for Troy.

But here delay held them. Agamemnon had chanced to kill a stag which was sacred to Diana, and the army was visited by pestilence, while a great calm kept the ships imprisoned. At length the Oracle made known the reason of this misfortune and demanded for atonement the maiden Iphigenia, Agamemnon's own daughter. In helpless grief the king consented to offer her up as a victim, and the maiden was brought ready for sacrifice. But at the last moment Diana caught her away in a cloud, leaving a white hind in her place, and carried her to Tauris in Scythia, there to serve as a priestess in the temple. In the mean time, her kinsfolk, who were at a loss to understand how she had disappeared, mourned her as dead. But Diana had accepted their child as an offering, and healing came to the army, and the winds blew again. So the ships set sail.

Meanwhile, in Troy across the sea, the aged Priam and Hecuba gave shelter to their son Paris and his stolen bride. They were not without misgivings as to these guests, but they made ready to defend their kindred and the citadel.

There were many heroes among the Trojans and their allies, brave and upright men, who little deserved that such reproach should be brought upon them by the guilt of Prince Paris. There were Aeneas and Deiphobus, Glaucus and Sarpedon, and Priam's most noble son Hector, chief of all the forces, and the very bulwark of Troy. These and many more were bitterly to regret the day that had brought Paris back to his home. But he had taken refuge with his own people, and the Trojans had to take up his cause against the hostile fleet that was coming across the sea.

Even the gods took sides. Juno and Athena, who had never forgiven the judgment of Paris, condemned all Troy with, him and favored the Greeks, as did also Poseidon, god of the sea. But Venus, true to her favorite, furthered the interests of the Trojans with all her power, and persuaded the warlike Mars to do likewise. Zeus and Apollo strove to be impartial, but they were yet to aid now one side, now another, according to the fortunes of the heroes whom they loved.

Over the sea came the great embassy of ships, sped hither safely by the god Poseidon; and the heroes made their camp on the plain before Troy. First of all Odysseus and King Menelaus himself went into the city and demanded that Fair Helen should be given back to her rightful husband. This the Trojans refused; and so began the siege of Troy.

III. THE WOODEN HORSE.

Nine years the Greeks laid siege to Troy, and Troy held out against every device. On both sides the lives of many heroes were spent, and they were forced to acknowledge each other enemies of great valor.

Sometimes the chief warriors fought in single combat, while the armies looked on, and the old men of Troy, with the women, came out to watch far off from the city walls. King Priam and Queen Hecuba would come, and Cassandra, sad with foreknowledge of their doom, and Andromache, the lovely young wife of Hector, with her little son whom the people called *The City King*. Sometimes Fair Helen came to look across the plain to the fellow-countrymen whom she had forsaken; and although she was the cause of all this war, the Trojans half forgave her when she passed by, because her beauty was like a spell, and warmed hard hearts as the sunshine mellows apples. So for nine years the Greeks plundered the neighboring towns, but the city Troy stood fast, and the Grecian ships waited with folded wings.

The half of that story cannot be told here, but in the tenth year of the war many things came to pass, and the end drew near. Of this tenth year alone, there are a score of tales. For the Greeks fell to quarrelling among themselves over the spoils of war, and the great Achilles left the camp in anger and refused to fight. Nothing would induce him to return, till his friend Patroclus was slain by Prince Hector. At that news, indeed, Achilles rose in great might and returned to the Greeks; and he went forth clad in armor that had been wrought for him by Vulcan, at the prayer of Thetis. By the river Scamander, near to Troy, he met and slew Hector, and afterwards dragged the hero's body after his chariot across the plain. How the aged Priam went alone by night to the tent of Achilles to ransom his son's body, and how Achilles relented, and moreover granted a truce for the funeral honors of his enemy,—all these things have been so nobly sung that they can never be fitly spoken.

Hector, the bulwark of Troy, had fallen, and the ruin of the city was at hand. Achilles himself did not long survive his triumph, and, ruthless as he was, he ill-deserved the manner of his death. He was treacherously slain by that Paris who would never have dared to meet him in the open field. Paris, though he had brought all this disaster upon Troy, had left the danger to his countrymen. But he lay in wait for Achilles in a temple sacred to Apollo, and from his hiding-place he sped a poisoned arrow at the hero. It pierced his ankle where the water of the Styx had not charmed him against wounds, and of that venom the great Achilles died. Paris himself died soon after by another poisoned arrow, but that was no long grief to anybody!

Still Troy held out, and the Greeks, who could not take it by force, pondered how they might take it by craft. At length, with the aid of Odysseus, they devised a plan.

A portion of the Grecian host broke up camp and set sail as if they were homeward bound; but, once out of sight, they anchored their ships behind a neighboring island. The rest of the army then fell to work upon a great image of a horse. They built it of wood, fitted and carved, and with a door so cunningly concealed that none might notice it. When it was finished, the horse looked like a prodigious idol; but it was hollow, skilfully pierced here and there, and so spacious that a band of men could lie hidden within and take no harm. Into this hiding-place went Odysseus, Menelaus, and the other chiefs, fully armed, and when the door was shut upon them, the rest of the Grecian army broke camp and went away.

Meanwhile, in Troy, the people had seen the departure of the ships, and the news had spread like wildfire. The great enemy had lost heart,—after ten years of war! Part of the army had gone,—the rest were going. Already the last of the ships had set sail, and the camp was deserted. The tents that had whitened the plain were gone like a frost before the sun. The war was over!

The whole city went wild with joy. Like one who has been a prisoner for many years, it flung off all restraint, and the people rose as a single man to test the truth of new liberty. The gates were thrown wide, and the Trojans—men, women, and children—thronged over the plain and into the empty camp of the enemy. There stood the Wooden Horse.

No one knew what it could be. Fearful at first, they gathered around it, as children gather around a live horse; they marvelled at its wondrous height and girth, and were for moving it into the city as a trophy of war.

At this, one man interposed,—Laocoön, a priest of Poseidon. "Take heed, citizens," said he. "Beware of all that comes from the Greeks. Have you fought them for ten years without learning their devices? This is some piece of treachery."

But there was another outcry in the crowd, and at that moment certain of the Trojans dragged forward a wretched man who wore the garments of a Greek. He seemed the sole remnant of the Grecian army, and as such they consented to spare his life, if he would tell them the truth.

Sinon, for this was the spy's name, said that he had been left behind by the malice of Odysseus, and he told them that the Greeks had built the Wooden Horse as an offering to Athena, and that they had made it so huge in order to keep it from being moved out of the camp, since it was destined to bring triumph to its possessors.

At this, the joy of the Trojans was redoubled, and they set their wits to find out how they might soonest drag the great horse across the plain and into the city to ensure victory. While they stood talking, two immense serpents rose out of the sea and made towards the camp. Some of the people took flight, others were transfixed with terror; but all, near and far, watched this new omen. Rearing their crests, the sea-serpents crossed the shore, swift, shining, terrible as a risen water-flood that descends upon a helpless little town. Straight through the crowd they swept, and seized the priest Laocoön where he stood, with his two sons, and wrapped them all round and round in fearful coils. There was no chance of escape. Father and sons perished together; and when the monsters had devoured the three men, into the sea they slipped again, leaving no trace of the horror.

The terrified Trojans saw an omen in this. To their minds, punishment had come upon Laocoön for his words against the Wooden Horse. Surely, it was sacred to the gods; he had spoken blasphemy, and had perished before their eyes. They flung his warning to the winds. They wreathed the horse with garlands, amid great acclaim; and then, all lending a hand, they dragged it, little by little, out of the camp and into the city of Troy. With the close of that victorious day, they gave up every memory of danger and made merry after ten years of privation.

That very night Sinon the spy opened the hidden door of the Wooden Horse, and in the darkness, Odysseus, Menelaus, and the other chiefs who had lain hidden there crept out and gave the signal to the Grecian army. For, under cover of night, those ships that had been moored behind the island had sailed back again, and the Greeks were come upon Troy.

Not a Trojan was on guard. The whole city was at feast when the enemy rose in its midst, and the warning of Laocoön was fulfilled.

Priam and his warriors fell by the sword, and their kingdom was plundered of all its fair possessions, women and children and treasure. Last of all, the city itself was burned to its very foundations.

Homeward sailed the Greeks, taking as royal captives poor Cassandra and Andromache and many another Trojan. And home at last went Fair Helen, the cause of all this sorrow, eager to be forgiven by her husband, King Menelaus. For she had awakened from the enchantment of Venus, and even before the death of Paris she had secretly longed for her home and kindred. Home to Sparta she came with the king after a long and stormy voyage, and there she lived and died the fairest of women.

But the kingdom of Troy was fallen. Nothing remained of all its glory but the glory of its dead heroes and fair women, and the ruins of its citadel by the river Scamander. There even now, beneath the foundations of later homes that were built and burned, built and burned, in the wars of a thousand years after, the ruins of ancient Troy lie hidden, like mouldered leaves deep under the new grass. And there, to this very day, men who love the story are delving after the dead city as you might search for a buried treasure.

THE HOUSE OF AGAMEMNON.

The Greeks had won back Fair Helen, and had burned the city of Troy behind them, but theirs was no triumphant voyage home. Many were driven far and wide before they saw their land again, and one who escaped such hardships came home to find a bitter welcome. This was the chief of all the hosts, Agamemnon, king of Mycenae and Argos. He it was who had offered his own daughter Iphigenia to appease the wrath of Diana before the ships could sail for Troy. An ominous leave-taking was his, and calamity was there to greet him home again.

He had entrusted the cares of the state to his cousin Aegisthus, commending also to his protection Queen Clytemnestra with her two remaining children, Electra and Orestes.

Now Clytemnestra was a sister of Helen of Troy, and a beautiful woman to see; but her heart was as evil as her face was fair. No sooner had her husband gone to the wars than she set up Aegisthus in his place, as if there were no other king of Argos. For years this faithless pair lived arrogantly in the face of the people, and controlled the affairs of the kingdom. But as time went by and the child Orestes grew to be a youth, Aegisthus feared lest the Argives should stand by their own prince, and drive him away as an usurper. He therefore planned the death of Orestes, and even won the consent of the queen, who was no gentle mother! But the princess Electra, suspecting their plot, secretly hurried her brother away to the court of King Strophius in Phocis, and so saved his life. She was not, however, to save a second victim.

The ten years of war went by, and the chief, Agamemnon, came home in triumph, heralded by all the Argives, who were as exultant over the return of their lawful king as over the fall of Troy. Into the city came the remnant of his own men, bearing the spoils of war, and, in the midst of a jubilant multitude, King Agamemnon sharing his chariot with the captive princess, Cassandra.

Queen Clytemnestra went out to greet him with every show of joy and triumph. She had a cloth of purple spread before the palace, that her husband might come with state into his home once more; and before all beholders she protested that the ten years of his absence had bereaved her of all happiness.

The unsuspicious king left his chariot and entered the palace; but the princess Cassandra hesitated and stood by in fear. Poor Cassandra! Her kindred were slain and the doom of her city was fulfilled, but the curse of prophecy still followed her. She felt the shadow of coming evil, and there before the door she recoiled, and cried out that there was blood in the air. At length, despairing of her fate, she too went in. Even while the Argives stood about the gates, pitying her madness, the prophecy came true.

Clytemnestra, like any anxious wife, had led the travel-worn king to a bath; and there, when he had laid by his arms, she and Aegisthus threw a net over him, as they would have snared any beast of prey, and slew him, defenceless. In the same hour Cassandra, too, fell into their hands, and they put an end to her warnings. So died the chief of the great army and his royal captive.

The murderers proclaimed themselves king and queen before all the people, and none dared rebel openly against such terrible authority. But Aegisthus was still uneasy at the thought that the Prince Orestes might return some day to avenge his father. Indeed, Electra had sent from time to time secret messages to Phocis, entreating her brother to come and take his rightful place, and save her from her cruel mother and Aegisthus. But there came to Argos one day a rumor that Orestes himself had died in Phocis, and the poor princess gave up all hope of peace; while Clytemnestra and Aegisthus made no secret of their relief, but even offered impious thanks in the temple, as if the gods were of their mind! They were soon undeceived.

Two young Phocians came to the palace with news of the last days of Orestes, so they said; and they were admitted to the presence of the king and queen. They were, in truth, Orestes himself and his friend Pylades (son of King Strophius), who had ventured safety and all to avenge Agamemnon. Then and there Orestes killed Aegisthus and Clytemnestra, and appeared before the Argives as their rightful prince.

But not even so did he find peace. In slaying Clytemnestra, wicked as she was, he had murdered his own mother, a deed hateful to gods and men. Day and night he was haunted by the Furies.

These dread sisters never leave Hades save to pursue and torture some guilty conscience. They wear black raiment, like the wings of a bat; their hair writhes with serpents fierce as remorse, and in their hands they carry flaming torches that make all shapes look greater and more fearful than they are. No sleep can soothe the mind of him they follow. They come between his eyes and the daylight; at night their torches drive away all comfortable darkness. Poor Orestes, though he had punished two murderers, felt that he was no less a murderer himself.

From land to land he wandered in despair that grew to madness, with one only comrade, the faithful Pylades, who was his very shadow. At length he took refuge in Athens, under the protection of Athena, and gave himself up to be tried by the court of the Areopagus. There he was acquitted; but not all the Furies left him, and at last he besought the Oracle of Apollo to befriend him.

"Go to Tauris, in Scythia," said the voice, "and bring from thence the image of Diana which fell from the heavens." So he set out with his Pylades and sailed to the shore of Scythia.

Now the Taurians were a savage people, who strove to honor Diana, to their rude minds, by sacrificing all the strangers that fell into their hands. There was a temple not far from the seaside, and its priestess was a Grecian maiden, one Iphigenia, who had miraculously appeared there years before, and was held in especial awe by Thoas, the king of the country round about. Sorely against her will, she had to hallow the victims offered at this shrine; and into her presence Orestes and Pylades were brought by the men who had seized them.

On learning that they were Grecians and Argives (for they withheld their names), the priestess was moved to the heart. She asked them many questions concerning the fate of Agamemnon, Clytemnestra, and the warriors against Troy, which they answered as best they could. At length she said that she would help one of them to escape, if he would swear to take a message from her to one in Argos.

"My friend shall bear it home," said Orestes. "As for me, I stay and endure my fate."

"Nay," said Pylades; "how can I swear? for I might lose this letter by shipwreck or some other mischance."

"Hear the message, then," said the high-priestess. "And thou wilt keep it by thee with thy life. To Orestes, son of Agamemnon, say Iphigenia, his sister, is dead indeed unto her parents, but not to him. Say that Diana has had charge over her these many years since she was snatched away at Aulis, and that she waits until her brother shall come to rescue her from this duty of bloodshed and take her home."

At these words their amazement knew no bounds. Orestes embraced his lost sister and told her all his story, and the three, breathless with eagerness, planned a way of escape.

The king of Tauris had already come to witness the sacrifice. But Iphigenia took in her hands the sacred image of Diana, and went out to tell him that the rites must be delayed. One of the strangers, said she, was guilty of the murder of his mother, the other sharing his crime; and these unworthy victims must be cleansed with pure sea-water before they could be offered to Diana. The sacred image had been desecrated by their touch, and that, too, must be solemnly purged by no other hands than hers.

To this the king consented. He remained to burn lustral fires in the temple; the people withdrew to their houses to escape pollution, and the priestess with her victims reached the seaside in safety.

Once there, with the sacred image which was to bring them good fortune, they hastened to the Grecian galley and put off from that desolate shore. So, with his new-found sister and his new hope, Orestes went over the seas to Argos, to rebuild the honor of the royal house.

THE ADVENTURES OF ODYSSEUS.

I. THE CURSE OF POLYPHEMUS.

Of all the heroes that wandered far and wide before they came to their homes again after the fall of Troy, none suffered so many hardships as Odysseus.

There was, indeed, one other man whose adventures have been likened to his, and this was Aeneas, a Trojan hero. He escaped from the burning city with a band of fugitives, his countrymen; and after years of peril and wandering he came to found a famous race in Italy. On the way, he found one hospitable resting-place in Carthage, where Queen Dido received him with great kindliness; and when he left her she took her own life, out of very grief.

But there were no other hardships such as beset Odysseus, between the burning of Troy and his return to Ithaca, west of the land of Greece. Ten years did he fight against Troy, but it was ten years more before he came to his home and his wife Penelope and his son Telemachus.

Now all these latter years of wandering fell to his lot because of Poseidon's anger against him. For Poseidon had favored the Grecian cause, and might well have sped home this man who had done so much to win the Grecian victory. But as evil destiny would have it, Odysseus mortally angered the god of the sea by blinding his son, the Cyclops Polyphemus. And thus it came to pass.

Odysseus set out from Troy with twelve good ships. He touched first at Ismarus, where his first misfortune took place, and in a skirmish with the natives he lost a number of men from each ship's crew. A storm then drove them to the land of the Lotus-Eaters, a wondrous people, kindly and content, who spend their lives in a day-dream and care for nothing else under the sun. No sooner had the sailors eaten of this magical lotus than they lost all their wish to go home, or to see their wives and children again. By main force,

Odysseus drove them back to the ships and saved them from the spell.

Thence they came one day to a beautiful strange island, a verdant place to see, deep with soft grass and well watered with springs. Here they ran the ships ashore, and took their rest and feasted for a day. But Odysseus looked across to the mainland, where he saw flocks and herds, and smoke going up softly from the homes of men; and he resolved to go across and find out what manner of people lived there. Accordingly, next morning, he took his own ship's company and they rowed across to the mainland.

Now, fair as the place was, there dwelt in it a race of giants, the Cyclopes, great rude creatures, having each but one eye, and that in the middle of his forehead. One of them was Polyphemus, the son of Poseidon. He lived by himself as a shepherd, and it was to his cave that Odysseus came, by some evil chance. It was an enormous grotto, big enough to house the giant and all his flocks, and it had a great courtyard without. But Odysseus, knowing nought of all this, chose out twelve men, and with a wallet of corn and a goatskin full of wine they left the ship and made a way to the cave, which they had seen from the water.

Much they wondered who might be the master of this strange house. Polyphemus was away with his sheep, but many lambs and kids were penned there, and the cavern was well stored with good-ly cheeses and cream and whey.

Without delay, the wearied men kindled a fire and sat down to eat such things as they found, till a great shadow came dark against the doorway, and they saw the Cyclops near at hand, returning with his flocks. In an instant they fled into the darkest corner of the cavern.

Polyphemus drove his flocks into the place and cast off from his shoulders a load of young trees for firewood. Then he lifted and set in the entrance of the cave a gigantic boulder of a door-stone. Not until he had milked the goats and ewes and stirred up the fire did his terrible one eye light upon the strangers.

"What are ye?" he roared then, "robbers or rovers?" And Odysseus alone had heart to answer.

"We are Achaeans of the army of Agamemnon," said he. "And by the will of Zeus we have lost our course, and are come to you as strangers. Forget not that Zeus has a care for such as we, strangers and suppliants."

Loud laughed the Cyclops at this. "You are a witless churl to bid me heed the gods!" said he. "I spare or kill to please myself and none other. But where is your cockle-shell that brought you hither?"

Then Odysseus answered craftily: "Alas, my ship is gone! Only I and my men escaped alive from the sea."

But Polyphemus, who had been looking them over with his one eye, seized two of the mariners and dashed them against the wall and made his evening meal of them, while their comrades stood by helpless. This done, he stretched himself through the cavern and slept all night long, taking no more heed of them than if they had been flies. No sleep came to the wretched seamen, for, even had they been able to slay him, they were powerless to move away the boulder from the door. So all night long Odysseus took thought how they might possibly escape.

At dawn the Cyclops woke, and his awakening was like a thunderstorm. Again he kindled the fire, again he milked the goats and ewes, and again he seized two of the king's comrades and served them up for his terrible repast. Then the savage shepherd drove his flocks out of the cave, only turning back to set the boulder in the doorway and pen up Odysseus and his men in their dismal lodging.

But the wise king had pondered well. In the sheepfold he had seen a mighty club of olive-wood, in size like the mast of a ship. As soon as the Cyclops was gone, Odysseus bade his men cut off a length of this club and sharpen it down to a point. This done, they hid it away under the earth that heaped the floor; and they waited in fear and torment for their chance of escape.

At sundown, home came the Cyclops. Just as he had done before, he drove in his flocks, barred the entrance, milked the goats and ewes, and made his meal of two more hapless men, while their fellows looked on with burning eyes. Then Odysseus stood forth, holding a bowl of the wine that he had brought with him; and, curbing his horror of Polyphemus, he spoke in friendly fashion:

"Drink, Cyclops, and prove our wine, such as it was, for all was lost with our ship save this. And no other man will ever bring you more, since you are such an ungentle host."

The Cyclops tasted the wine and laughed with delight so that the cave shook. "Ho, this is a rare drink!" said he. "I never tasted milk so good, nor whey, nor grape-juice either. Give me the rest, and tell me your name, that I may thank you for it."

Twice and thrice Odysseus poured the wine and the Cyclops drank it off; then he answered: "Since you ask it, Cyclops, my name is Noman."

"And I will give you this for your wine, Noman," said the Cyclops; "you shall be eaten last of all!"

As he spoke his head drooped, for his wits were clouded with drink, and he sank heavily out of his seat and lay prone, stretched along the floor of the cavern. His great eye shut and he fell asleep.

Odysseus thrust the stake under the ashes till it was glowing hot; and his fellows stood by him, ready to venture all. Then together they lifted the club and drove it straight into the eye of Polyphemus and turned it around and about.

The Cyclops gave a horrible cry, and, thrusting away the brand, he called on all his fellow-giants near and far. Odysseus and his men hid in the uttermost corners of the cave, but they heard the resounding steps of the Cyclopes who were roused, and their shouts as they called, "What ails thee, Polyphemus? Art thou slain? Who has done thee any hurt?"

"Noman!" roared the blinded Cyclops; "Noman is here to slay me by treachery."

"Then if no man hath hurt thee," they called again, "let us sleep." And away they went to their homes once more.

But Polyphemus lifted away the boulder from the door and sat there in the entrance, groaning with pain and stretching forth his hands to feel if any one were near. Then, while he sat in double darkness, with the light of his eye gone out, Odysseus bound together the rams of the flock, three by three, in such wise that every three should save one of his comrades. For underneath the mid ram of each group a man clung, grasping his shaggy fleece; and the rams on each side guarded him from discovery. Odysseus himself chose out the greatest ram and laid hold of his fleece and clung beneath his shaggy body, face upward.

Now, when dawn came, the rams hastened out to pasture, and Polyphemus felt of their backs as they huddled along together; but he knew not that every three held a man bound securely. Last of all came the kingly ram that was dearest to his rude heart, and he bore the King of Ithaca. Once free of the cave, Odysseus and his fellows loosed their hold and took flight, driving the rams in haste to the ship, where, without delay, they greeted their comrades and went aboard.

But as they pushed from shore, Odysseus could not refrain from hailing the Cyclops with taunts, and at the sound of that voice Polyphemus came forth from his cave and hurled a great rock after the ship. It missed and upheaved the water like an earthquake. Again Odysseus called, saying: "Cyclops, if any shall ask who blinded thine eye, say that it was Odysseus, son of Laertes of Ithaca."

Then Polyphemus groaned and cried: "An Oracle foretold it, but I waited for some man of might who should overcome me by his valor,—not a weakling! And now"—he lifted his hands and prayed,—"Father Poseidon, my father, look upon Odysseus, the son of Laertes of Ithaca, and grant me this revenge,—let him never see Ithaca again! Yet, if he must, may he come late, without a friend, after long wandering, to find evil abiding by his hearth!"

So he spoke and hurled another rock after them, but the ship outstripped it, and sped by to the island where the other good ships waited for Odysseus. Together they put out from land and hastened on their homeward voyage.

But Poseidon, who is lord of the sea, had heard the prayer of his son, and that homeward voyage was to wear through ten years more, with storm and irksome calms and misadventure.

II. THE WANDERING OF ODYSSEUS.

Now Odysseus and his men sailed on and on till they came to Aeolia, where dwells the king of the winds, and here they came nigh to good fortune.

Aeolus received them kindly, and at their going he secretly gave to Odysseus a leathern bag in which all contrary winds were tied up securely, that only the favoring west wind might speed them to Ithaca. Nine days the ships went gladly before the wind, and on the tenth day they had sight of Ithaca, lying like a low cloud in the west. Then, so near his haven, the happy Odysseus gave up to his weariness and fell asleep, for he had never left the helm. But while he slept his men saw the leathern bag that he kept by him, and, in the belief that it was full of treasure, they opened it. Out rushed the ill-winds!

In an instant the sea was covered with white caps; the waves rose mountain high; the poor ships struggled against the tyranny of the gale and gave way. Back they were driven,—back, farther and farther; and when Odysseus woke, Ithaca was gone from sight, as if it had indeed been only a low cloud in the west!

Straight to the island of Aeolus they were driven once more. But when the king learned what greed and treachery had wasted his good gift, he would give them nothing more. "Surely thou must be a man hated of the gods, Odysseus," he said, "for misfortune bears thee company. Depart now; I may not help thee."

So, with a heavy heart, Odysseus and his men departed. For many days they rowed against a dead calm, until at length they came to the land of the Laestrygonians. And, to cut a piteous tale short, these giants destroyed all their fleet save one ship,—that of Odysseus himself, and in this he made escape to the island of Circe. What befell there, how the greedy seamen were turned into swine and turned back into men, and how the sorceress came to befriend Odysseus,—all this has been related.

There in Aeaea the voyagers stayed a year before Circe would let them go. But at length she bade Odysseus seek the region of Hades, and ask of the sage Tiresias how he might ever return to Ithaca. How Odysseus followed this counsel, none may know; but by some mysterious journey, and with the aid of a spell, he came to the borders of Hades. There he saw and spoke with many renowned Shades, old and young, even his own friends who had fallen on the plain of Troy. Achilles he saw, Patroclus and Ajax and Agamemnon, still grieving over the treachery of his wife. He saw, too, the phantom of Heracles, who lives with honor among the gods, and has for his wife Hebe, the daughter of Zeus and Juno. But though he would have talked with the heroes for a year and more, he sought out Tiresias.

"The anger of Poseidon follows thee," said the sage. "Wherefore, Odysseus, thy return is yet far off. But take heed when thou art come to Thrinacia, where the sacred kine of the Sun have their pastures. Do them no hurt, and thou shalt yet come home. *But if they be harmed in any wise*, ruin shall come upon thy men; and even if thou escape, thou shalt come home to find strange men devouring thy substance and wooing thy wife."

With this word in his mind, Odysseus departed and came once more to Aeaea. There he tarried but a little time, till Circe had told him all the dangers that beset his way. Many a good counsel and crafty warning did she give him against the Sirens that charm with their singing, and against the monster Scylla and the whirlpool Charybdis, and the Clashing Rocks, and the cattle of the Sun. So the king and his men set out from the island of Aeaea.

Now very soon they came to the Sirens who sing so sweetly that they lure to death every man who listens. For straightway he is mad to be with them where they sing; and alas for the man that would fly without wings!

But when the ship drew near the Sirens' island, Odysseus did as Circe had taught him. He bade all his shipmates stop up their ears with moulded wax, so that they could not hear. He alone kept his hearing: but he had himself lashed to the mast so that he could in no wise move, and he forbade them to loose him, however he might plead, under the spell of the Sirens.

As they sailed near, his soul gave way. He heard a wild sweetness coaxing the air, as a minstrel coaxes the harp; and there, close by, were the Sirens sitting in a blooming meadow that hid the bones of men. Beautiful, winning maidens they looked; and they sang, entreating Odysseus by name to listen and abide and rest. Their voices were golden-sweet above the sound of wind and wave, like drops of amber floating on the tide; and for all his wisdom, Odysseus strained at his bonds and begged his men to let him go free. But they, deaf alike to the song and the sorcery, rowed harder than ever. At length, song and island faded in the distance. Odysseus came to his wits once more, and his men loosed his bonds and set him free.

But they were close upon new dangers. No sooner had they avoided the Clashing Rocks (by a device of Circe's) than they came to a perilous strait. On one hand they saw the whirlpool where, beneath a hollow fig-tree, Charybdis sucks down the sea horribly. And, while they sought to escape her, on the other hand monstrous Scylla upreared from the cave, snatched six of their company with her six long necks, and devoured them even while they called upon Odysseus to save them.

So, with bitter peril, the ship passed by and came to the island of Thrinacia; and here are goodly pastures for the flocks and herds of the Sun. Odysseus, who feared lest his men might forget the warning of Tiresias, was very loath to land. But the sailors were weary and worn to the verge of mutiny, and they swore, moreover, that they would never lay hands on the sacred kine. So they landed, thinking to depart next day. But with the next day came a tempest that blew for a month without ceasing, so that they were forced to beach the ship and live on the island with their store of corn and wine. When that was gone they had to hunt and fish, and it happened that, while Odysseus was absent in the woods one day, his shipmates broke their oath. "For," said they, "when we are once more in Ithaca we will make amends to Helios with sacrifice. But let us rather drown than waste to death with hunger." So they drove off the best of the cattle of the Sun and slew them. When the king returned, he found them at their fateful banquet; but it was too late to save them from the wrath of the gods.

As soon as they were fairly embarked once more, the Sun ceased to shine. The sea rose high, the thunderbolt of Zeus struck that ship, and all its company was scattered abroad upon the waters. Not one was left save Odysseus. He clung to a fragment of his last ship, and so he drifted, borne here and there, and lashed by wind and wave, until he was washed up on the strand of the island Ogygia, the home of the nymph Calypso. He was not to leave this haven for seven years.

Here, after ten years of war and two of wandering, he found a kindly welcome. The enchanted island was full of wonders, and the nymph Calypso was more than mortal fair, and would have been glad to marry the hero; yet he pined for Ithaca. Nothing could win his heart away from his own country and his own wife Penelope, nothing but Lethe itself, and that no man may drink till he dies.

So for seven years Calypso strove to make him forget his longing with ease and pleasant living and soft raiment. Day by day she sang to him while she broidered her web with gold; and her voice was like a golden strand that twines in and out of silence, making it beautiful. She even promised that she would make him immortal, if he would stay and be content; but he was heartsick for home.

At last his sorrow touched even the heart of Athena in heaven, for she loved his wisdom and his many devices. So she besought Zeus and all the other gods until they consented to shield Odysseus from the anger of Poseidon. Hermes himself bound on his winged sandals and flew down to Ogygia, where he found Calypso at her spinning. After many words, the nymph consented to give up her captive, for she was kind of heart, and all her graces had not availed to make him forget his home. With her help, Odysseus built a raft and set out upon his lonely voyage,—the only man remaining out of twelve good ships that had left Troy nigh unto ten years before.

The sea roughened against him, but (to shorten a tale of great peril) after many days, sore spent and tempest-tossed, he came to the land of the Phaeacians, a land dear to the immortal gods, abounding in gifts of harvest and vintage, in godlike men and lovely women.

Here the shipwrecked king met the princess Nausicaa by the seaside, as she played ball with her maidens; and she, when she had heard of his plight, gave him food and raiment, and bade him follow her home. So he followed her to the palace of King Alcinous and Queen Arete, and abode with them, kindly refreshed, and honored with feasting and games and song. But it came to pass, as the minstrel sang before them of the Trojan War and the Wooden Horse, that Odysseus wept over the story, it was written so deep in his own heart. Then for the first time he told them his true name and all his trials.

They would gladly have kept so great a man with them forever, but they had no heart to keep him longer from his home; so they bade him farewell and set him upon one of their magical ships, with many gifts of gold and silver, and sent him on his way.

Wonderful seamen are the Phaeacians. The ocean is to them as air to the bird, — the best path for a swift journey! Odysseus was glad enough to trust the way to them, and no sooner had they set out than a sweet sleep fell upon his eyelids. But the good ship sped like any bee that knows the way home. In a marvellous short time they came even to the shore of the kingdom of Ithaca.

While Odysseus was still sleeping, unconscious of his good fortune, the Phaeacians lifted him from the ship with kindly joy and laid him upon his own shore; and beside him they set the gifts of gold and silver and fair work of the loom. So they departed; and thus it was that Odysseus came to Ithaca after twenty years.

III. THE HOME-COMING.

Now all these twenty years, in the island of Ithaca, Penelope had watched for her husband's return. At first with high hopes and then in doubt and sorrow (when news of the great war came by some traveller), she had waited, eager and constant as a young bride. But now the war was long past; her young son Telemachus had come to manhood; and as for Odysseus, she knew not whether he was alive or dead.

For years there had been trouble in Ithaca. It was left a kingdom without a king, and Penelope was fair and wise. So suitors came from all the islands round about to beg her hand in marriage, since many loved the queen and as many more loved her possessions, and desired to rule over them. Moreover, every one thought or said that King Odysseus must be dead. Neither Penelope nor her aged father-in-law Laertes could rid the place of these troublesome suitors. Some were nobles and some were adventurers, but they all thronged the palace like a pest of crickets, and devoured the wealth of the kingdom with feasts in honor of Penelope and themselves and everybody else; and they besought the queen to choose a husband from their number.

For a long time she would hear none of this; but they grew so clamorous in their suit that she had to put them off with craft. For she saw that there would be danger to her country, and her son, and herself, unless Odysseus came home some day and turned the suitors out of doors. She therefore spoke them fair, and gave them some hope of her marriage, to make peace.

"Ye princely wooers," she said, "now I believe that the king Odysseus, my husband, must long since have perished in a strange land; and I have bethought me once more of marriage. Have patience, therefore, till I shall have finished the web that I am weaving. For it is a royal shroud that I must make against the day that Laertes may die (the father of my lord and husband). This is the way of my people," said she; "and when the web is done, I will choose another king for Ithaca."

She had set up in the hall a great loom, and day by day she wrought there at the web, for she was a marvellous spinner, patient as Arachne, but dear to Athena. All day long she would weave, but every night in secret she would unravel what she had wrought in the daytime, so that the web might never be done. For although she believed her dear husband to be dead, yet her hope would put forth buds again and again, just as spring, that seems to die each year, will come again. So she ever looked to see Odysseus coming.

Three years and more she held off the suitors with this wile, and they never perceived it. For, being men, they knew nothing of women's handicraft. It was all alike a marvel to them, both the beauty of the web and this endless toil in the making! As for Penelope, all day long she wove; but at night she would unravel her work and weep bitterly, because she had another web to weave and another day to watch, all for nothing, since Odysseus never came. In the fourth year, though, a faithless servant betrayed this secret to the wooers, and there came an end to peace and the web, too!

Matters grew worse and worse. Telemachus set out to find his father, and the poor queen was left without husband or son. But the suitors continued to live about the palace like so many princes, and to make merry on the wealth of Odysseus, while he was being driven from land to land and wreck to wreck. So it came true, that prophecy that, if the herds of the Sun were harmed, Odysseus should reach his home alone in evil plight to find Sorrow in his own household. But in the end he was to drive her forth.

Now, when Odysseus woke, he did not know his own country. Gone were the Phaeacians and their ship; only the gifts beside him told him that he had not dreamed. While he looked about, bewildered, Athena, in the guise of a young countryman, came to his aid, and told him where he was. Then, smiling upon his amazement and joy, she shone forth in her own form, and warned him not to hasten home, since the palace was filled with the insolent suitors of Penelope, whose heart waited empty for him as the nest for the bird.

Moreover, Athena changed his shape into that of an aged pilgrim, and led him to the hut of a certain swineherd, Eumaeus, his old and faithful servant. This man received the king kindly, taking him for a travel-worn wayfarer, and told him all the news of the palace, and the suitors and the poor queen, who was ever ready to hear the idle tales of any traveller if he had aught to tell of King Odysseus.

Now who should come to the hut at this time but the prince Telemachus, whom Athena had hastened safely home from his quest! Eumaeus received his young master with great joy, but the heart of Odysseus was nigh to bursting, for he had never seen his son since he left him, an infant, for the Trojan War. When Eumaeus left them together, he made himself known; and for that moment Athena gave him back his kingly looks, so that Telemachus saw him with exultation, and they two wept over each other for joy.

By this time news of her son's return had come to Penelope, and she was almost happy, not knowing that the suitors were plotting to kill Telemachus. Home he came, and he hastened to assure his mother that he had heard good news of Odysseus; though, for the safety of all, he did not tell her that Odysseus was in Ithaca.

Meanwhile Eumaeus and his aged pilgrim came to the city and the palace gates. They were talking to a goatherd there, when an old hound that lay in the dust-heap near by pricked up his ears and stirred his tail feebly as at a well-known voice. He was the faithful Argus, named after a monster of many eyes that once served Juno as a watchman. Indeed, when the creature was slain, Juno had his eyes set in the feathers of her pet peacocks, and there they glisten to this day. But the end of this Argus was very different. Once the pride of the king's heart, he was now so old and infirm that he could barely move; but though his master had come home in the guise of a strange beggar, he knew the voice, and he alone, after twenty years. Odysseus, seeing him, could barely restrain his tears; but the poor old hound, as if he had lived but to welcome his master home, died that very same day.

Into the palace hall went the swineherd and the pilgrim, among the suitors who were feasting there. Now how Odysseus begged a portion of meat and was shamefully insulted by these men, how he saw his own wife and hid his joy and sorrow, but told her news of himself as any beggar might,—all these things are better sung than spoken. It is a long story.

But the end was near. The suitors had demanded the queen's choice, and once more the constant Penelope tried to put it off. She took from her safe treasure-chamber the great bow of Odysseus, and she promised that she would marry that one of the suitors who should send his arrow through twelve rings ranged in a line. All other weapons were taken away by the care of Telemachus; there was nothing but the great bow and quiver. And when all was ready, Penelope went away to her chamber to weep.

But, first of all, no one could string the bow. Suitor after suitor tried and failed. The sturdy wood stood unbent against the strongest. Last of all, Odysseus begged leave to try, and was laughed to scorn. Telemachus, however, as if for courtesy's sake, gave him the bow; and the strange beggar bent it easily, adjusted the cord, and before any could stay his hand he sped the arrow from the string. Singing with triumph, it flew straight through the twelve rings and quivered in the mark!

"Now for another mark!" cried Odysseus in the king's own voice. He turned upon the most evil-hearted suitor. Another arrow hissed and struck, and the man fell pierced.

Telemachus sprang to his father's side, Eumaeus stood by him, and the fighting was short and bitter. One by one they slew those insolent suitors; for the right was theirs, and Athena stood by them, and the time was come. Every one of the false-hearted wooers they laid low, and every corrupt servant in that house; then they made the place clean and fair again.

But the old nurse Eurycleia hastened up to Queen Penelope, where she sat in fear and wonder, crying, "Odysseus is returned! Come and see with thine own eyes!"

After twenty years of false tales, the poor queen could not believe her ears. She came down into the hall bewildered, and looked at the stranger as one walking in a dream. Even when Athena had given him back his youth and kingly looks, she stood in doubt, so that her own son reproached her and Odysseus was grieved in spirit.

But when he drew near and called her by her name, entreating her by all the tokens that she alone knew, her heart woke up and sang like a brook set free in spring! She knew him then for her husband Odysseus, come home at last.

Surely that was happiness enough to last them ever after.